DC SUPER HERO ORIGIN STORIES

By Michael Robin

with Noah Smith and Nathanael Katz

downtown bookworks

downtown bookworks

Downtown Bookworks Inc.
New York, New York
www.downtownbookworks.com

Designed by Georgia Rucker
Printed in China, January 2022
10 9 8 7 6 5 4 3 2 1

Batman created by Bob Kane with Bill Finger

Superman created by Jerry Siegel and Joe Shuster
By special arrangement with the Jerry Siegel family

Supergirl based on characters created by Jerry Siegel and Joe Shuster
By special arrangement with the Jerry Siegel Family

Wonder Woman created by William Moulton Marston

Aquaman created by Paul Norris and Mort Weisinger

CONTENTS

SUPERMAN

Baby Kal-El was born on a planet called Krypton. His mother, Lara, was an astronaut. His father, Jor-El, was a scientist. Krypton had two moons and orbited a red sun far from Earth. It was not a stable planet. It became clear to Jor-El that the entire planet was going to blow up—and soon. He and Lara built an escape rocket as quickly as they could. They had only enough time to build something big enough to hold their baby son. Heartbroken but happy they could save his life, they sent him off to Earth.

When John and Martha Kent saw something fiery streak through the sky, they followed it and discovered a small rocket . . . with a baby sleeping inside. They took that baby home to their farm the same day. They'd always wanted a child and almost couldn't believe their luck. They named him Clark, and they loved him and raised him as their own.

Clark liked growing up on the farm with wide open spaces to play in and tractors to ride. And he loved his parents. But as they all soon discovered, he was no ordinary farm boy. Earth's yellow sun gave him super-human strength. Not only could young Clark lift up a truck with one hand, but he could run through the fields at super-speed. He had X-ray vision (he could see right through the walls of the barn). He even had heat vision. He could melt pots and pans just by looking at them. And . . . he could fly!

Being Kryptonian made Superman more powerful than anyone on Earth. But he had one weakness. When his home planet exploded into millions of radioactive pieces, some of those pieces of rock, called Kryptonite, fell to Earth. If Superman came near any of those green crystal-like rocks, he would lose all of his strength.

When he was a kid, Clark kept his special powers secret from his friends in Smallville. When he grew up and moved to Metropolis, he started to work at a newspaper called the *Daily Planet*. None of the other reporters knew his secret either. As a journalist, Clark Kent could keep track of what was going on in the world and figure out where help was needed most.

Then, he would slip out of his glasses and tie and into his blue Superman suit. Whenever he was needed, Superman saved the day!

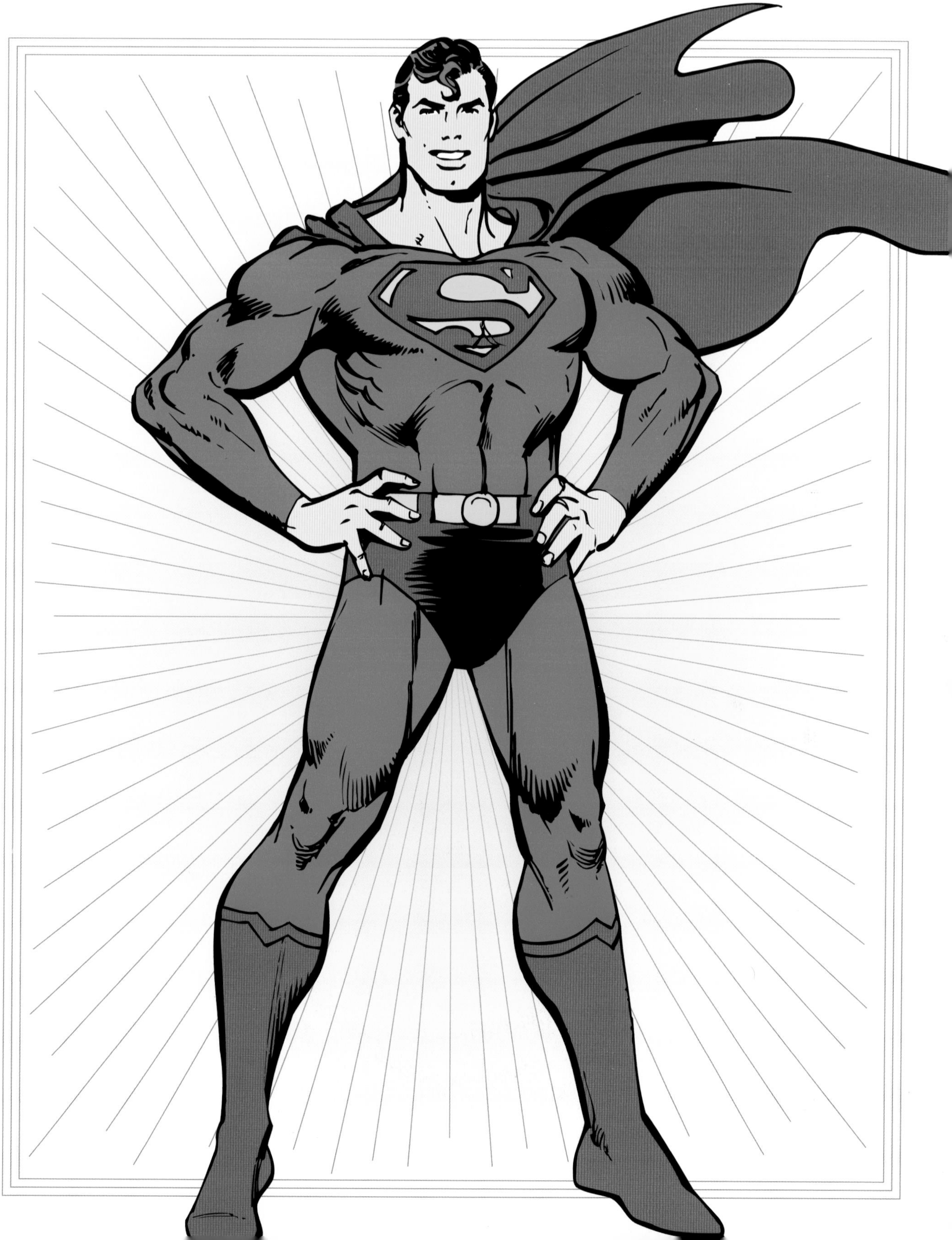

SUPERGIRL

When their planet exploded, the citizens of Argo City felt like the luckiest people on Krypton. Most of the planet was destroyed or transformed into deadly Kryptonite by the explosion. But the ground underneath Argo City broke off from the rest of the planet in one giant chunk and floated into space like a city-sized asteroid!

A scientist named Zor-El built a metal floor to keep out the deadly Kryptonite rays from below. And above, the city was protected by a giant dome with plenty of air inside. High-tech food machines made food, as they always had, so nobody inside the dome went hungry.

As the city journeyed through the galaxy, people moved on with their lives within its dome. Zor-El fell in love with a wise judge named Alura, and they had a daughter named Kara. Kara never knew any life outside the dome.

Then one day, a swarm of meteors crashed into Argo City and punched holes in the metal sheets that protected it. The people began to get sick. Zor-El and Alura decided to send Kara someplace safe. Zor-El knew that his brother, Jor-El, had sent Kara's cousin Kal-El to Earth. He thought that maybe Kara would be safe there too. With tears in her eyes, a teenage Kara climbed aboard a rocket and waved goodbye.

She landed in a strange place where she didn't understand the language. Earth technology seemed slow and old-fashioned compared to Kryptonian technology. Strangest of all, Kara now had the strength to break anything she touched—Earth's yellow sun had given her extraordinary powers. She could also fly! She had X-ray vision and heat vision. The only thing she couldn't do was fit in.

Kara did find her cousin, known as Superman on Earth, and he helped her adjust to her new life. A group called the Department of Extranormal Operations (DEO) was looking after Kara as well. The DEO knew that she had superpowers and gave her a secret identity—Kara Danvers. They even assigned two agents, Eliza and Jeremiah, to be her Earth mom and dad. They sent her to National City Technical High School. Slowly, Kara made friends and settled into her life on Earth. And over time, she used her superpowers, like her cousin Superman, to make her new home planet a safer place.

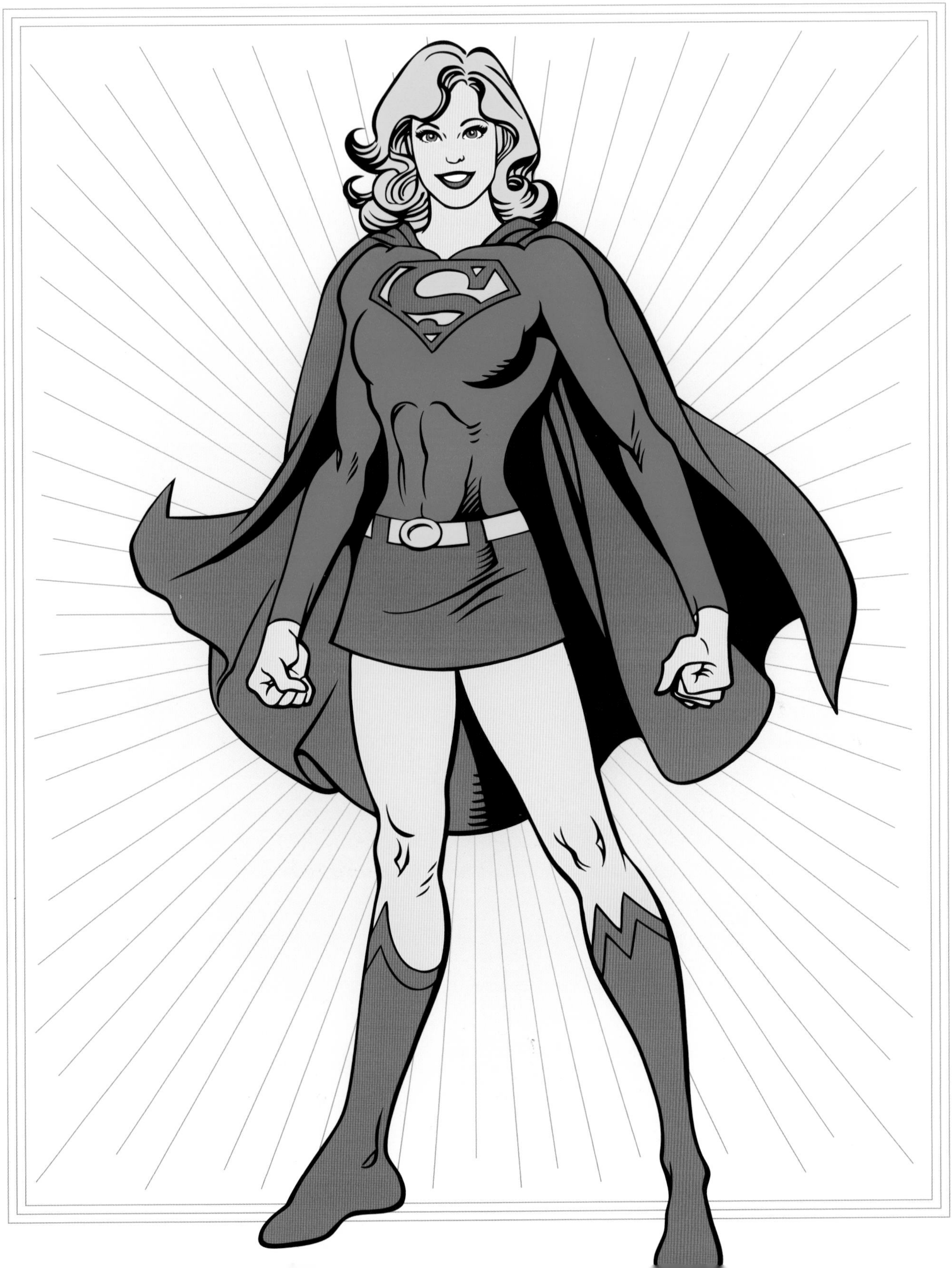

BLACK LIGHTNING

People in the crime-ridden streets of Metropolis lived in constant fear, without hope that they could ever make their lives or their city any safer. But Jefferson Pierce believed that he could make his hometown a better place.

Jefferson was an athlete. He practiced for hours every day to qualify for the Olympics. He made it—in the most difficult competition of all—the decathlon. This is a combination of 10 different grueling track-and-field events. Jefferson faced talented challengers from around the world. By the time they had completed their 10th event, Jefferson was the winner. Wearing his gold medal, he proudly proved that a poor kid from Metropolis could accomplish anything.

Jefferson was every bit as smart as he was athletic. He studied at school and was a passionate reader. He even wrote poetry:

> *Justice, like lightning, should ever appear*
> *to some men hope, to other men fear.*

Jefferson became a teacher in Metropolis to bring his love of learning to his community. He was determined to inspire students who knew only crime and despair. It wasn't easy, when gangsters ruled the streets and corrupt city leaders were in charge. Metropolis needed justice. And the need was too big for one man to tackle.

But it turned out that Jefferson was more powerful than even an Olympic athlete. Born with powers of electrokinesis, he could generate and manipulate his own electricity. He had kept this gift hidden for long enough. He could shoot lightning bolts from his hands, and he could protect himself with an electromagnetic force field if needed. He could stun criminals in their tracks with an electric charge. He was very careful with his powers, using them only to become the force of justice he had written about in his poem. While he continued to teach high school and broaden minds by day, at night he made it possible for his students, their families, and their neighbors to sleep soundly.

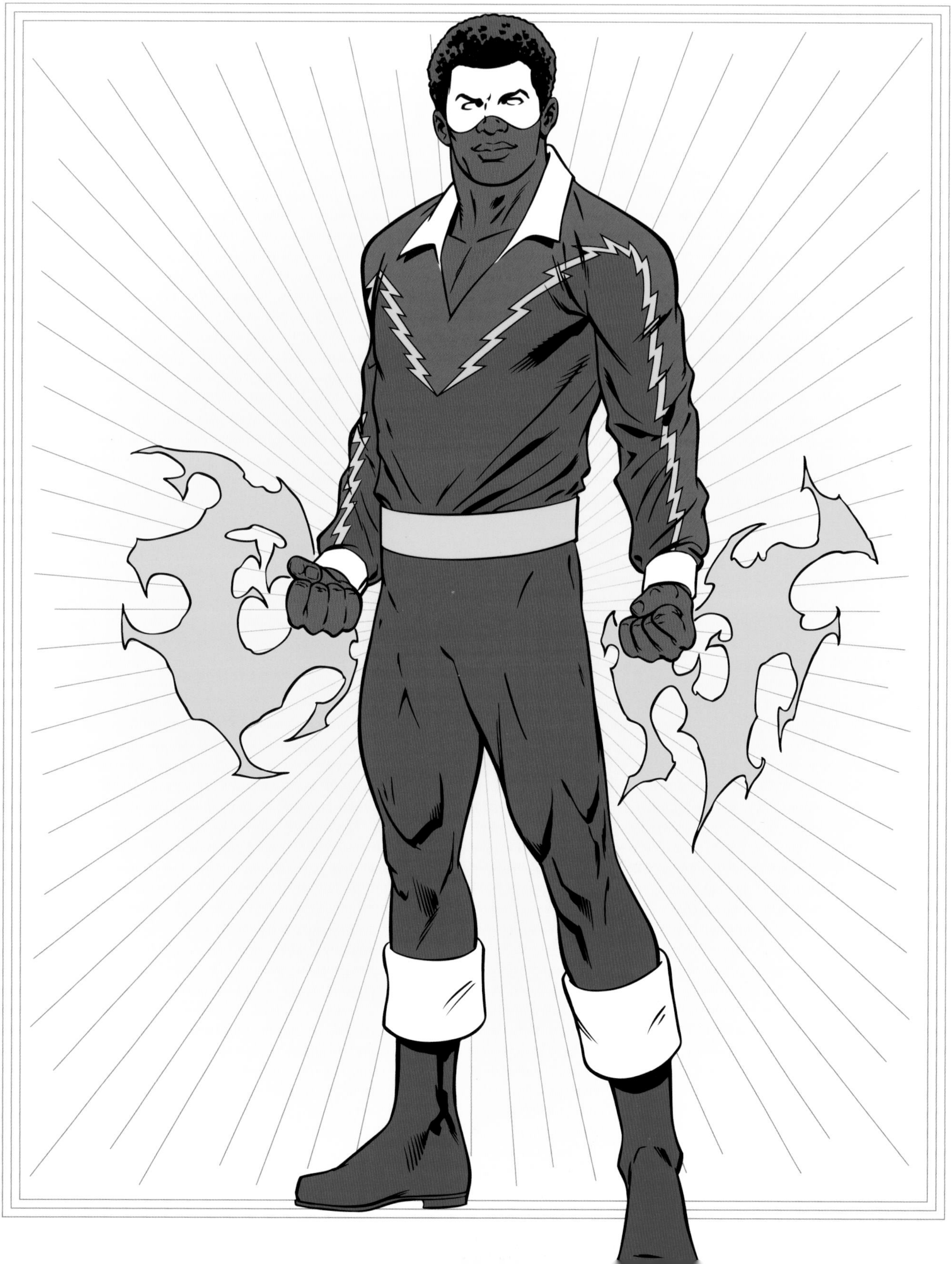

BATMAN

Bruce Wayne had everything an eight-year-old could want. He lived on the outskirts of Gotham City in a huge house—a mansion, really—called Wayne Manor. He had the best toys and vacations that money could buy. He even had a butler named Alfred Pennyworth. Best of all, Bruce had two loving parents, Thomas and Martha Wayne. Bruce's parents were as famous for their good deeds as for their billions. They used their money to help the needy. Bruce loved them and looked up to them.

One day, the family went to a movie in town. Bruce had a wonderful time. He and his parents started to walk home afterwards. Suddenly, from out of the shadows jumped a petty thief. He wanted Martha's pearl necklace. Thomas fought back and there was a terrible struggle. When it was over, Bruce's parents were no longer alive. The thief was gone.

Without his parents, it didn't matter that he lived in a giant house filled with toys. Bruce felt like he had lost everything. Alfred took care of him, making sure Bruce had hot meals and did his schoolwork. But Bruce was sad and angry. He couldn't stop thinking about why good people should have to live in fear. He didn't understand why some people were just . . . bad.

Finally, Bruce realized his parents wouldn't want him to give up. He vowed to fight for a world in which good people could feel safe. Bruce would make the criminals afraid—of him. He trained day and night to strengthen his muscles and mind. When he was old enough, he traveled all over the world to learn as much as he could. He studied martial arts so he could fight. He learned about technology so he could create the most advanced computer and equipment. He became a brilliant scientist and expert fighter.

When he returned to Wayne Manor, he pretended to be a boring millionaire during the day. By night, he and Alfred went to work in the bat-filled caves underneath his home. Together, they built a Batcomputer and a Batmobile. They designed amazing tools like a Batarang for stopping criminals in their tracks, and a Batrope for scaling tall buildings.

Bruce took his Super Hero name from the bats who kept him company while he worked at night, and a legend was born. The good people of Gotham City were grateful to Batman—and the criminals feared him. One night at a time, he tried to make things right in the world.

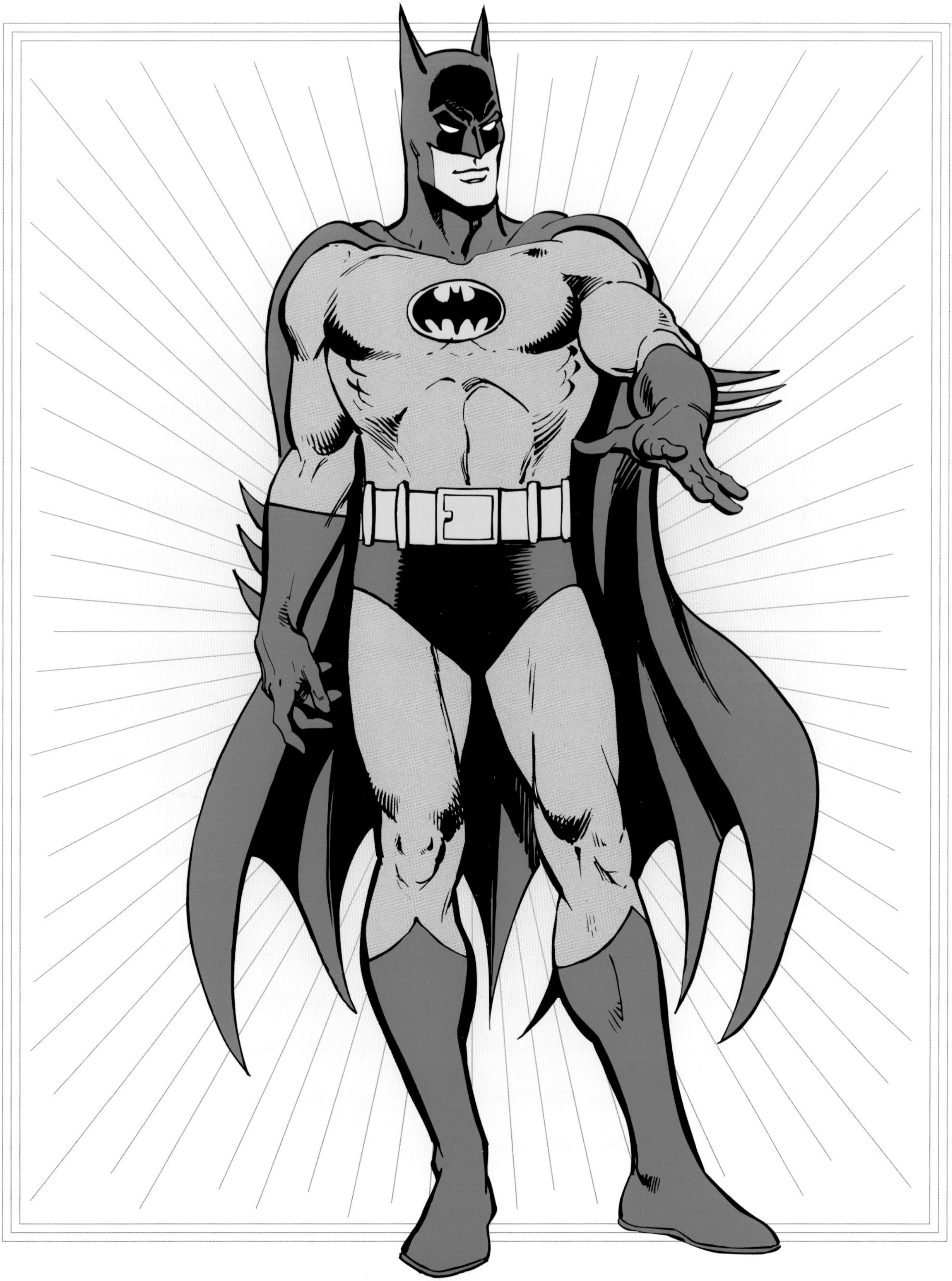

BATGIRL

Barbara Gordon dreamed she'd grow up to be a crime fighter. She wanted to be just like her father, Gotham City police commissioner James Gordon. But her dad said no—police work was too dangerous. He told Barbara to find a safer dream instead.

Barbara was a top student and took a job as a librarian at the Gotham City Public Library. It seemed about as far from crime fighting as you could get. She loved to read, and she enjoyed the quiet of the library. But every time she closed her eyes, Barbara still fought villains in her dreams.

Then one day Barbara discovered that her father had a secret. He was friends with Batman! As she spied on her dad's meeting with the Caped Crusader, Barbara felt inspired. Her father could stop her from being a police officer, but he couldn't stop her from being a Super Hero!

Barbara became a Super Hero the same way she'd become a straight-A student—by studying hard. She hacked her dad's computer to learn about criminals and their habits. She read city maps and police reports. She practiced martial arts for hours and hours every day. Finally she made herself a costume like Batman's, complete with a bat-symbol on the front. When she was ready and suited up, Batgirl took to the rooftops.

She soon ran into Batman's sidekick, Robin, on patrol. Almost instantly, they got along. Both were young and liked to have a little fun while catching villains. But Robin knew Batman wouldn't be happy about this new Bat in Gotham City. And sure enough, when Barbara first met Batman, his famous frown was deep. She asked to join him. He said no—that Super Hero work was too dangerous. But Barbara didn't back down. She said that she was going to be Batgirl with or without him.

Batman was impressed. Not many people stood up to him. So he decided to give her a chance. He met with her night after night to test her. He tested her reflexes and her martial arts moves. He challenged her mind and her computer skills. Barbara got knocked down a lot. But she always got up. She also learned from her mistakes. Finally Batman had to admit it. Batgirl was a true Super Hero. He let her join the Batman Family. Really, what choice did he have?

Every night (and many days) Barbara Gordon got to live her dream of keeping Gotham City safe.

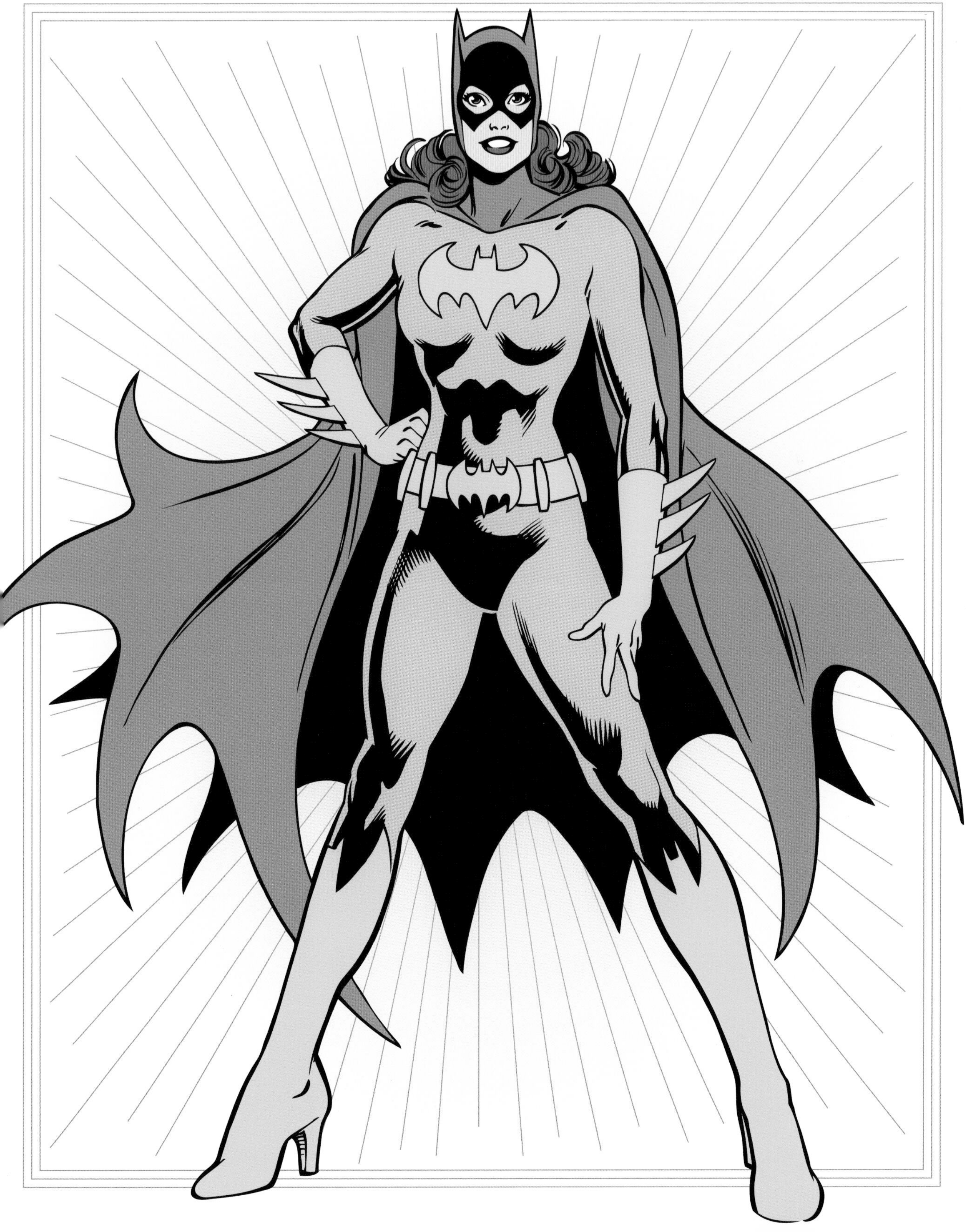

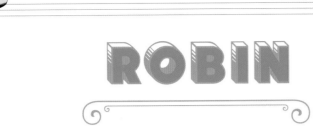

ROBIN

Before he even learned to walk, Dick Grayson learned to swing from a flying trapeze. His parents, John and Mary Grayson, were famous circus acrobats and when he was still a child, Dick joined the family act. The "Flying Graysons" became the main attraction at Haly's Circus. People came from all around to see them perform heart-stopping stunts high overhead without a net. Dick grew up traveling from town to town in the company of clowns, trained animals, sword swallowers, and strongmen. It was a magical childhood.

Everything changed one day when Dick was eight years old. While he was getting ready for a show, he overheard two gangsters demand money from the circus owner. The owner refused and the gangsters went away. But when no one was looking, they cut the Flying Graysons' trapeze ropes. During the next performance, the ropes snapped. Dick was spared but his parents fell to their doom.

In the audience that night was Bruce Wayne (secretly Batman). Bruce had also lost his parents at a young age, and he had never stopped feeling angry and sad. He didn't want Dick Grayson to grow up feeling the same way. Batman decided to help.

To Batman's surprise, Dick wanted more than his help—he wanted to be his crime-fighting partner! Batman wanted to say no—being a Super Hero is dangerous. But Dick's troubled face touched his heart. That very night by candlelight, Dick swore an oath to always follow a righteous path. Then his training began: boxing, jiujitsu, detective work, and more. Years later, he even learned to drive the Batmobile! It was exhausting, but Dick was a natural. His circus acrobatics turned out to be the perfect Super Hero skill. Finally, they made a costume and Robin, the Boy Wonder, was born.

Batman and Robin became the most famous Super Hero partners of all time. The first thing they did was take down the criminals who'd harmed Robin's parents. Soon the whole Gotham City underworld learned to fear this new "Dynamic Duo." But Robin was always more than just a sidekick. In time, Bruce Wayne adopted Dick Grayson and the two officially became father and son. Brought together by tragedy, Batman and Robin found a new family when they found each other.

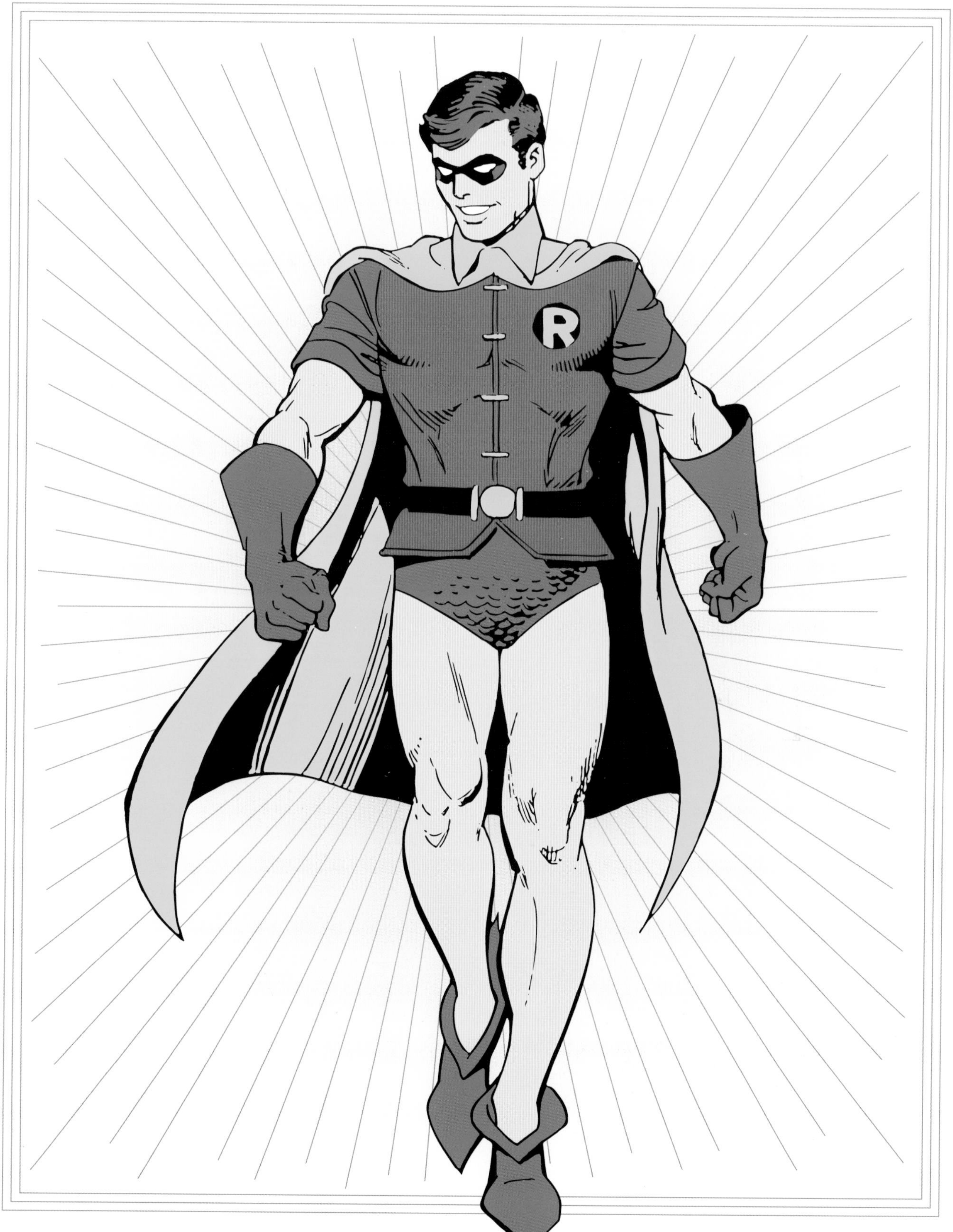
R

RAVEN

For most of her life, everyone told Raven she was bad. She was born in a beautiful city called Azarath. It was protected by a magic spell. Evil could not enter the city. Raven's mother, Arella, was a priestess of peace.

There was only one problem—Raven's father was an all-powerful demon lord named Trigon. Her mother had met him when she was a troubled girl in Gotham City. When Arella realized Trigon's true nature, she ran away to Azarath. The day Raven was born, Azarath's skies darkened. Something was wrong. Evil had found a way in after all.

Some Azarathians didn't want to let Raven stay. They were afraid she would ruin their paradise. Raven knew exactly how everyone felt about her. When people around her felt joy, anger, love—Raven felt those same feelings. She was *empathic*. So she knew she was feared and mistrusted.

She could also control other people's feelings. This made her dangerous. The Azarathians taught Raven to stop feeling, to cut herself off from other people. They said it was the only way to hold back her evil nature. Raven believed what people said about her. She worried she was a threat to everyone she cared about. She often thought about running away.

One day Raven opened the Great Door between Azarath and the outside world. Waiting on the other side was her father, the demon-lord Trigon. He acted like he cared about her. He told her she was much more powerful than the Azarathians knew. He showed her how to release her soul-self, a great bird made of shadows that gave Raven extraordinary powers. Trigon explained to Raven that she was evil just like him.

Raven realized that her father was right—and wrong. Yes, there was great power and great evil inside her. But she could choose her own path. Raven also realized that the Azarathians were wrong too. Shutting off her feelings wasn't the answer. It was time to leave Azarath. And the first thing she had to do was to fight Trigon to keep him out of her life.

Raven knew that her life would be a constant battle between good and evil, between wild emotions and total control. Eventually, she made her way to Earth where she became friends with other young Super Heroes and together, they formed the Teen Titans. Having friends who understood her and worked with her made every battle easier. And Raven finally knew she was strong enough to win.

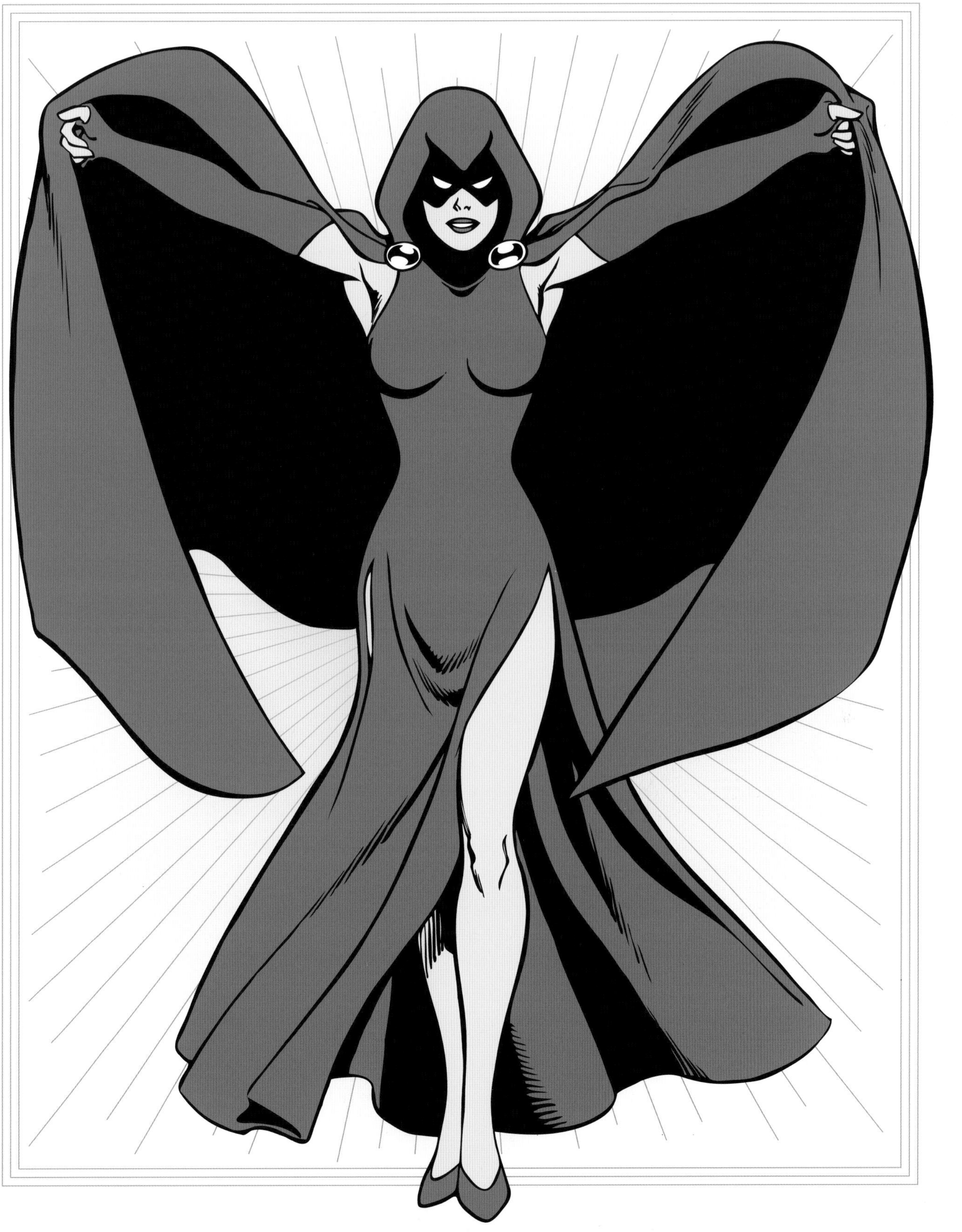

CYBORG

Victor Stone's parents, Silas and Elinore, were scientists. Like many little boys, Victor's parents loved him a lot. Unlike any other boys, one of the ways Victor's parents showed their love was by enhancing his brain. Though Victor was naturally smart, his parents used advanced technology to make him even smarter. By the time he was in middle school, he had a genius-level IQ. He was expected to be a star student.

But Victor didn't want to perform in school just to please his parents. He was not happy that they had altered his brain. He stopped doing his homework and even skipped school sometimes. He wanted to play football instead, and he was a great athlete.

One night Victor went to see his parents at S.T.A.R. Labs, where they worked. He felt bad for letting them down and went to apologize. His timing could not have been worse! His father had just opened a portal (like a door) to another dimension. A terrible, violent creature from this other universe attacked Victor's mother, and then Victor. The creature seriously injured Victor before Silas could send it back where it came from.

There was only one way for Silas to save his son. At S.T.A.R. Labs, some scientists were working on cybernetics (robotic parts). Silas used these robotic body parts in order to save Victor's life. He replaced half of Victor's brain with a robot brain. Victor was given robotic arms so strong that he could lift an airplane without straining himself! His robotic eye enabled him to see a ladybug from miles away. His human organs were protected by a metal shell that shielded him from heat, electricity, and brutal weather conditions. His robotic legs gave him super-speed.

In many ways, Victor was better—stronger, faster, smarter even. But when he woke up after the attack, he was shocked to see that he was no longer himself. He was part-robot—which meant that he was only part-human. He was angry and sad for a long time.

Eventually, he realized that he had been given a second chance. With this new life and extraordinary powers, he chose a hero's path. He joined the Teen Titans—a group of kids his age who were also different, and very powerful. And together with Robin, Bumblebee, Raven, Starfire, and Beast Boy, they used their powers to help others.

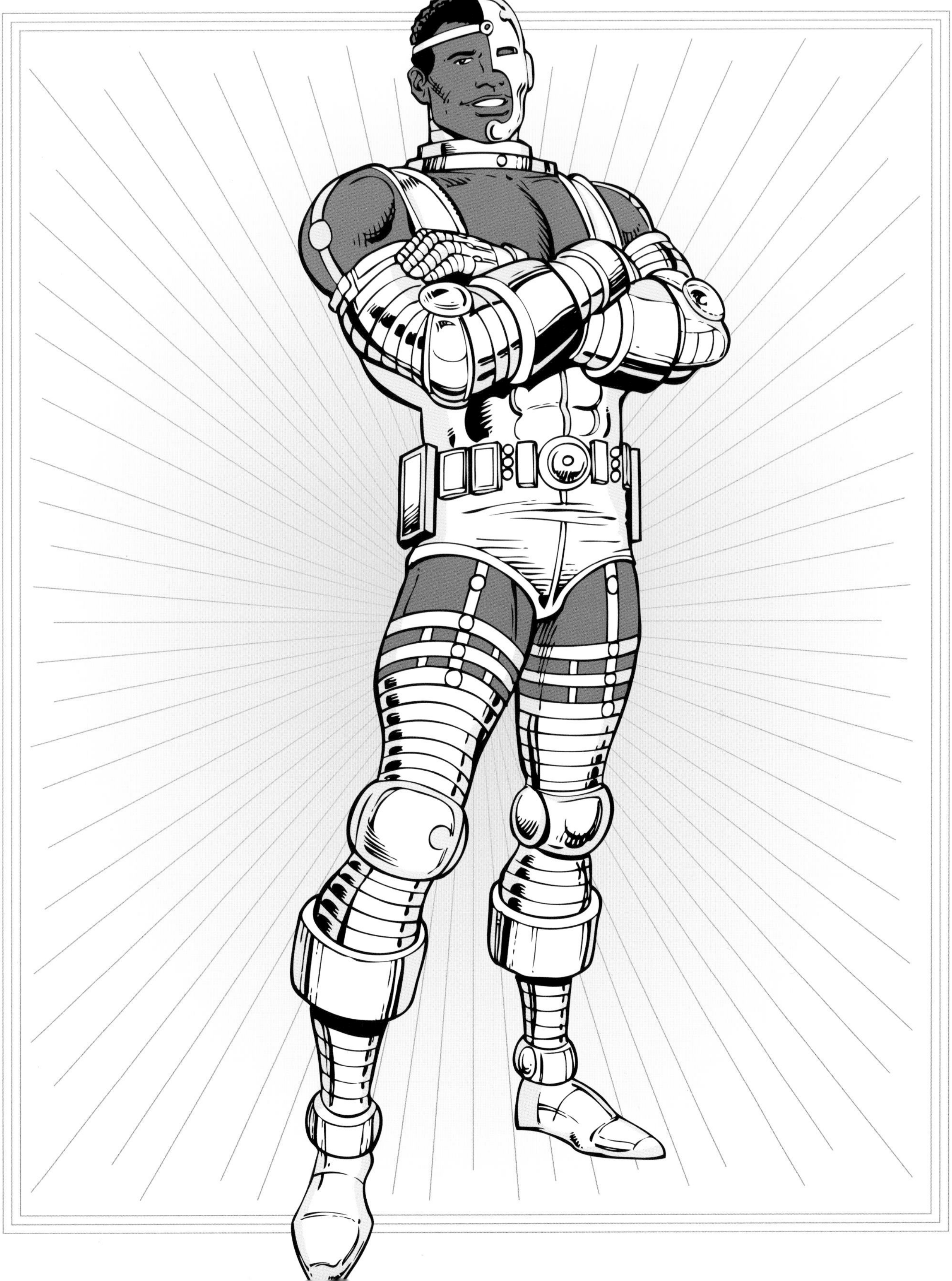

STARFIRE

Koriand'r and her sister Komand'r were both princesses on the Planet Tamaran. Koriand'r was next in line for the throne—and when she was about to be queen, her sister became angry and jealous and turned on her. Komand'r allowed the evil Citadel to take over their planet rather than watch her sister take her rightful throne. Koriand'r fled. She could fly great distances through the galaxy. And she found her way to Earth.

One of the Tamaraneans' gifts is that they can understand every language as soon as they touch someone who speaks that language. On Earth, Koriand'r learned how to speak English from Robin. Tamaraneans also absorb ultraviolet energy from the light around them. This stored energy gave Koriand'r her super-strength and toughness, and allowed her to fly at tremendous speeds. She developed the power to shoot energy blasts called "starbolts" from her hands.

Her new Earth friends called her Kori. They realized she had some incredible powers and invited her to join the Teen Titans on their adventures. She took on the Super Hero name Starfire and got to work right away with Robin, Cyborg, Raven, Bumblebee, and Beast Boy. Together, they went to Tamaran, where they overthrew the Citadel and Komand'r to free the peaceful Tamaranean people.

As bold a warrior as Starfire is, she has much more love in her heart than anger. She remains hopeful that someday she and her sister will reunite as friends. In the meantime, she made Earth her home, and her mission is to keep its people safe.

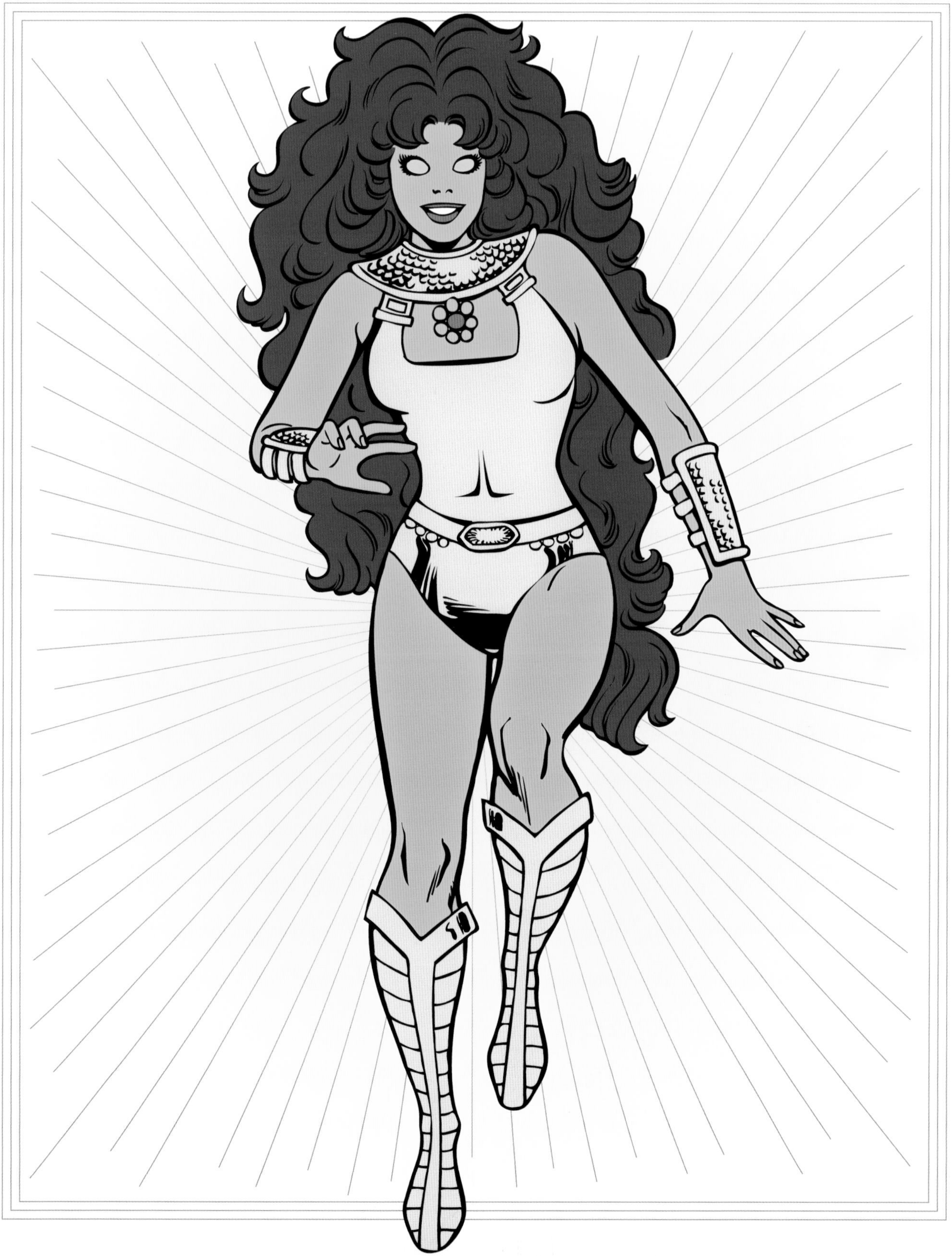

BEAST BOY

Garfield Logan loved animals. He lived with his parents deep in the West African rain forest. There were wild animals all around their home—and inside of it too! Gar's parents were scientists. They were inventing a way to bring back extinct creatures. They called their new process "reverse evolution." They worked day and night. Gar had a lot of time to himself. So the animals of the forest and the laboratory became his best friends.

Unfortunately, Gar caught a disease, Sakutia, from one of his animal friends. The illness had no cure. No creature on Earth ever survived Sakutia except for one— the West African green monkey. Desperate to save Gar, his parents used "reverse evolution" to turn him into a green monkey. It worked! Gar's new monkey body fought off the disease. When his parents changed him back into a human they had a surprise— Gar's skin, hair, and eyes had turned green.

Soon, they would learn that those weren't the only changes in Gar. One day, while he was playing in a tree, he looked down and saw a big snake slither towards his mother. It was a deadly poisonous black mamba! Gar's mind raced. *What was a black mamba's greatest enemy? A mongoose.* As the thought crossed his mind, Gar's body transformed into a green mongoose! He leaped from the tree and saved his mother from the snake.

Gar had gained the power to change into any animal he knew about. He could be as enormous as an elephant or as tiny as a mouse. He could be a bird flying on air currents or a fish swimming through the sea. He could even turn into extinct animals, like a woolly mammoth or a saber-toothed tiger. No matter what size, shape, or form he took, Gar always stayed green.

Gar's parents worried that greedy people might try to use him for selfish purposes, so they tried to keep his animal powers secret. There would be many such people in Gar's future. But they never stopped the boy who loved animals from soaring, swimming, running, and roaring with the creatures of the forest.

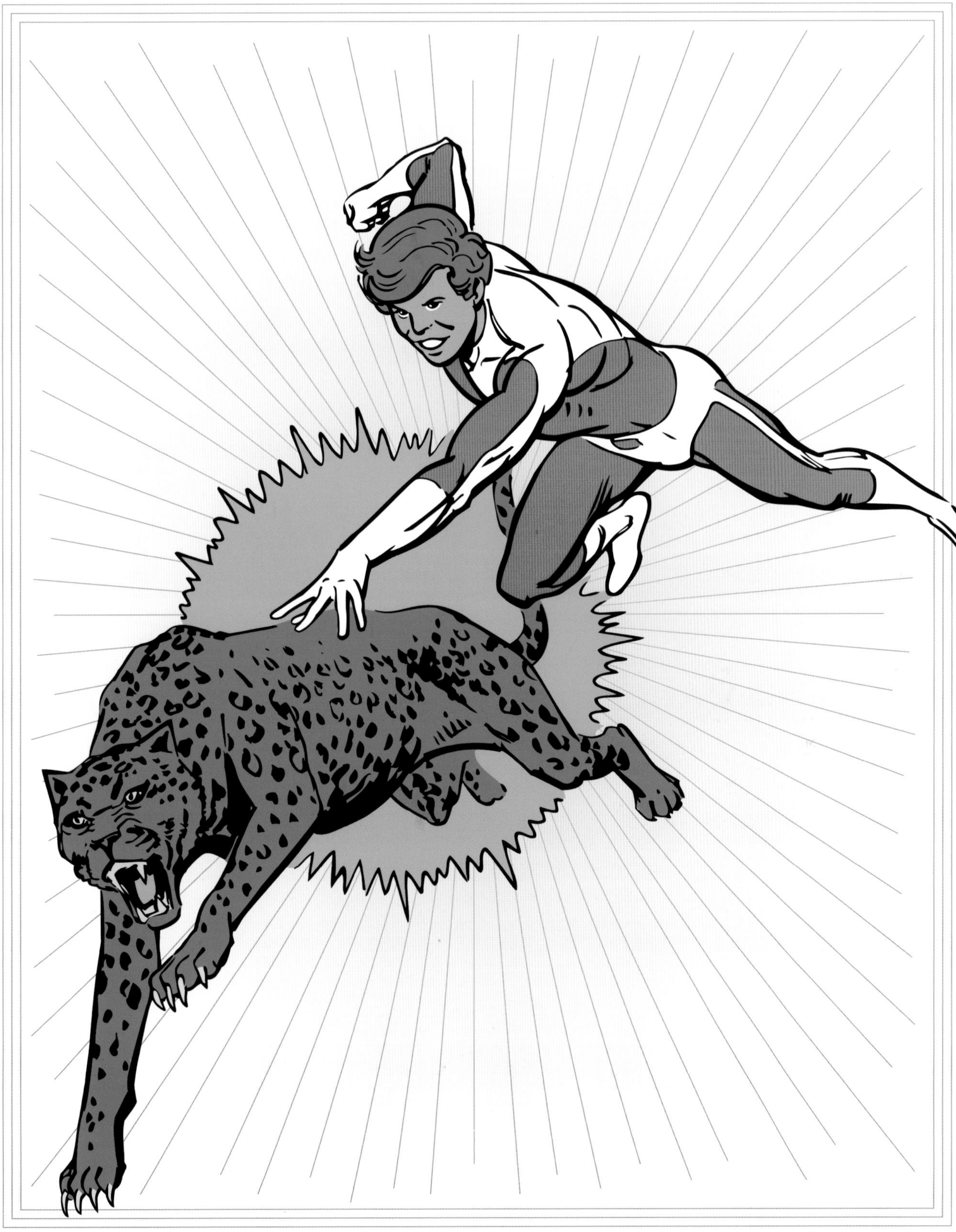

BUMBLEBEE

Karen Beecher thought she had all the answers. She was a brilliant scientist. She had creativity and determination to spare. So when her boyfriend Mal complained about problems at work, she decided to try to help.

Mal didn't have a regular job. He was a Super Hero called Hornblower. He had recently joined a group of young Super Heroes called the Teen Titans, alongside heroes like Robin and Raven. Karen thought being a Teen Titan would make Mal happy, but all he did was complain. He worried that the other Super Heroes didn't take him seriously. Karen urged Mal to stand up for himself. She said that anybody could be a Teen Titan if they really wanted to be. She had no idea how true her words would turn out to be!

Karen decided to teach both Mal and the Teen Titans a lesson. She would pretend to be a Super-Villain and attack Mal in front of his teammates. Then she would let him win.

Karen invented a Super-Villain named Bumblebee. Karen gave her all to everything she did, including this prank. She built a high-tech battle suit with all of the capabilities she imagined a superhero would need: flight, strength, armor, a loud sonic buzz, a tail-mounted stinger beam—even a honey blaster! Best of all, this suit enabled her to shrink to the size of a bee. At that size, Karen easily snuck into Teen Titans headquarters.

When it was time to "attack" Mal and let him impress the other heroes, things did not go according to plan. Karen immediately took out Mal with one shot from her honey blaster. She didn't make Mal look so good after all. But she did give the Teen Titans a chance to show him that they liked him. They leaped into action to help him. Suddenly, Karen was in for a tough battle! She turned out to be a worthy opponent, successfully fighting off the entire team. She finally knocked them down with a sonic buzz and escaped.

Karen's secret didn't last long. Mal had recognized Bumblebee's voice. Together they went to the Titans and told them the truth. The Titans weren't mad. Instead, they were impressed. They even invited Karen to join the team, and she happily accepted. Bumblebee, the *real* Super Hero, went on to do great things with her Teen Titan friends and on her own.

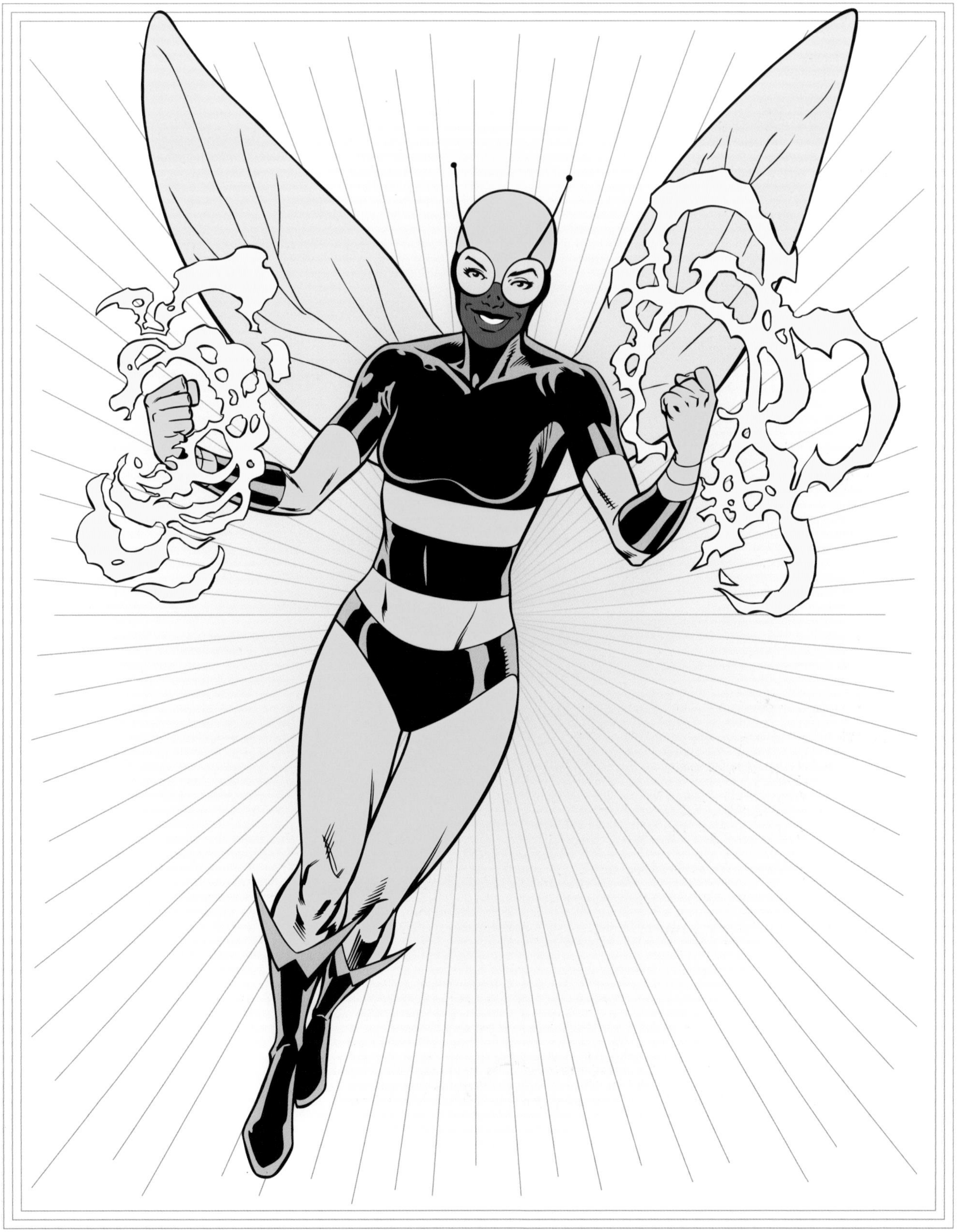

WONDER WOMAN

Wonder Woman's story begins with her mother, Queen Hippolyta, on an island called Themyscira. The island is hidden and protected by a spell. The Amazons—a group of powerful women—went there so they could live in a peaceful place free of violence.

Hippolyta led a happy life on her beautiful island with its sparkling waterfalls and lush greenery. Still, she wanted a daughter. One day, she scooped up some sand from the beach and molded it into a baby. Zeus, the god, gave the baby life. At the same time, he gave her the powers of the gods—super-strength, great speed, flight, and the ability to heal.

The little girl, Diana, grew up as a princess among the Amazons who were strong, gifted fighters—although they believed in peace. They knew that the they might have to defend their island and their way of life, so they were prepared. Hippolyta's sister, Antiope, was the swiftest, fiercest, and most skilled of them all. She taught Diana everything she knew.

One day, a man flying a small plane crash-landed on the island. The man was a soldier named Steve Trevor, and he told the Amazons that the world was at war, and that he had been fighting in a battle before he landed there. Hippolyta decided that one of the Amazons should leave the island to set an example for others, to show them how to live peacefully. She held a contest to see who was the strongest, fastest, and bravest. She did not want her daughter to leave, so she did not allow Diana to participate in the contest. But that didn't stop Diana. She wore a disguise, entered the contest, and won!

Diana knew that if she left Themyscira, she might not be able to return. But she was willing to take the risk to bring peace to the world. The Amazons were as smart as they were strong, and they had developed very advanced technology. When Diana left the island, she flew on an Invisible Jet. She took a Golden Lasso with her. Also known as the Lasso of Truth, it had magical powers. If she caught someone in her lasso, that person would be forced to tell the truth. With her lasso and a mission to spread peace, Diana left her home and became known to the rest of the world as Wonder Woman.

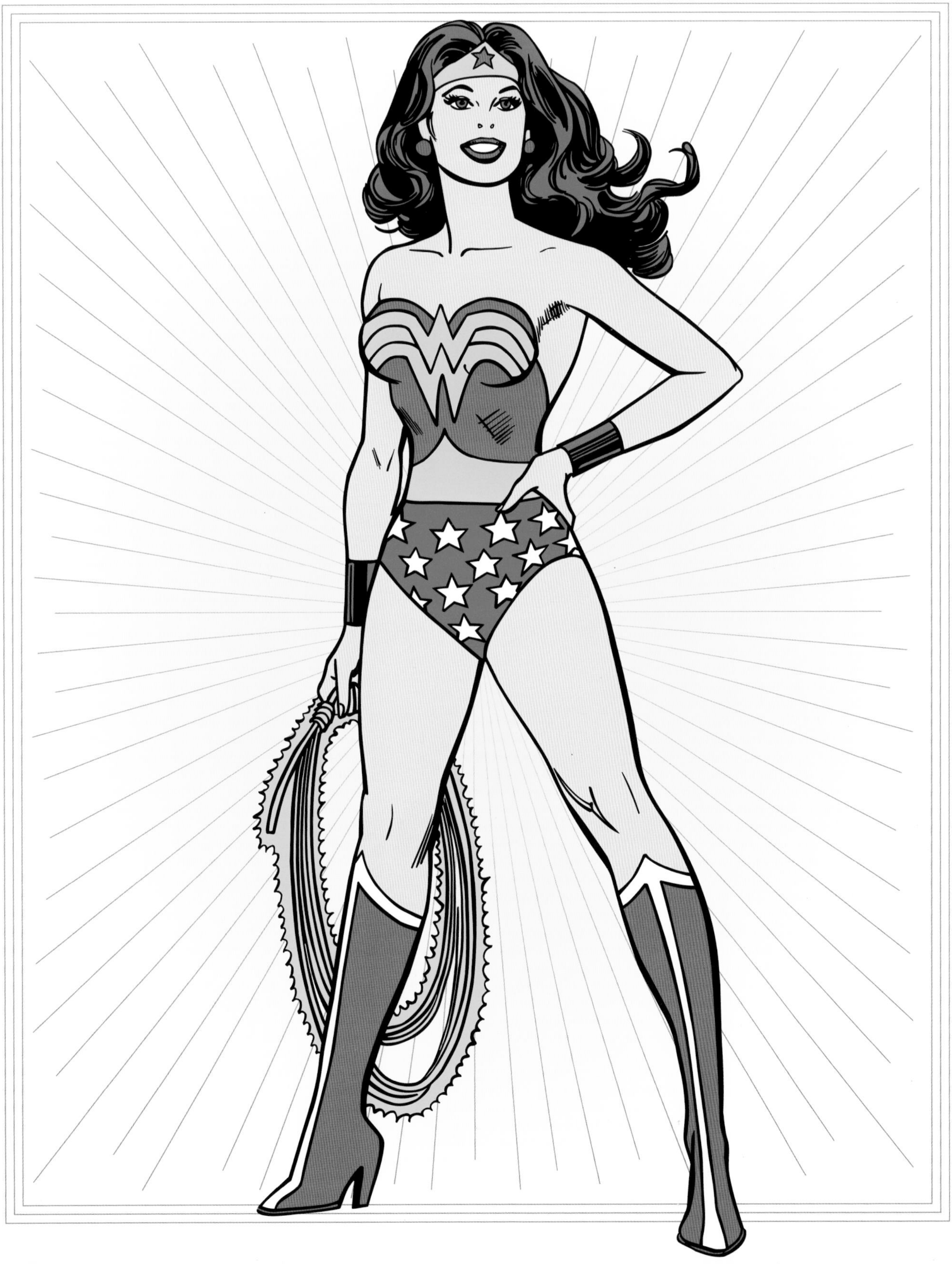

NUBIA

Though many people know Princess Diana, who became Wonder Woman, Queen Hippolyta actually molded two daughters out of sand! Diana had a twin sister named Nubia. While Diana grew up in Themyscira under the care and love of Hippolyta and the other Amazons, Nubia was kidnapped as a baby by Ares, the god of war. Hippolyta loved her daughter Nubia every bit as much as she loved Diana. None of the other Amazons knew that she had a second daughter, or that she grieved that long-lost daughter every single day.

Ares took baby Nubia to Floating Island with the hopes of raising a warrior. As the god of war, he loved a good fight! The Floating Island was the opposite of Themyscira. Only men lived there—except for Nubia. Ares used all his force to try to control Nubia's mind. He wanted to destroy the Amazons and he was determined to use Nubia's strength and superpowers to do so. After all, Nubia was just as strong, as fast, and as wise as Diana. She *could* overpower the Amazons, if she tried. Ares convinced Nubia that the Amazons were her enemy. He was sure that Nubia could win any battle with her powers and skills, and his training.

Nubia learned to be an extraordinary fighter, but she did not actually want to fight. It didn't feel right to her. The day came when Ares sent Nubia to Themyscira to battle her "enemy," Diana. Nubia was dressed from head to toe in an armored suit. She fought hard and well, and she proved herself to be a worthy opponent. The Amazons were amazed by her skills. Nubia almost defeated Diana . . . but she could not bring herself to finish the battle. Something inside of her held her back. She didn't want to be fighting against the Amazons. She was much too smart to fight a senseless war. Without actually knowing that Diana was her sister, she felt a sisterhood with the peace-loving Amazons.

As Nubia walked away, Hippolyta thanked her for ending the battle and asked her to remove her armored mask. When Nubia revealed her face, Hippolyta could not believe her eyes. She recognized her now grown daughter and began to sob.

Nubia, her mother Hippolyta, and her sister Diana banished Ares from Themyscira. Then Nubia vowed to join her Amazon sisters in spreading peace throughout the world. Although she did not get to know and live with them until she was a woman, Nubia would later become a powerful leader of the Amazons in her rightful homeland.

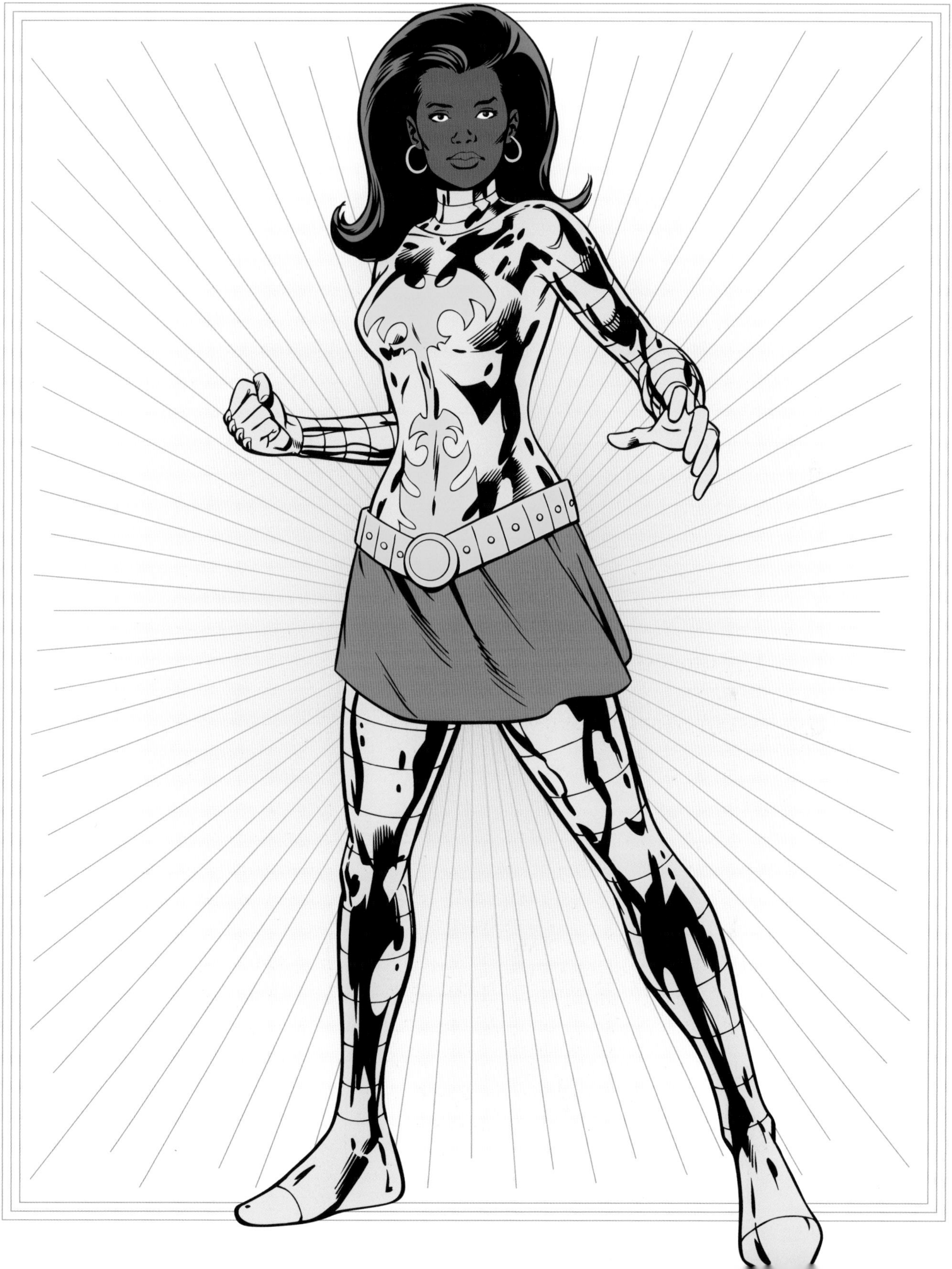

AQUAMAN

Tom Curry the lighthouse keeper lived a simple life. He watched the waves outside Amnesty Bay, Maine, with only the gulls for company. His lonely days came to an end when a terrible storm threw him into the sea. A mysterious woman named Atlanna pulled him from the water and nursed him back to health. Tom and Atlanna fell in love and had a son, whom they named Arthur.

The family's good fortune would not last, however. Atlanna had a secret—she was the runaway queen of the underwater kingdom of Atlantis! It wasn't long before Atlantean soldiers found Atlanna and tried to force her to return home. Atlanna defeated the soldiers but realized that her family would never be safe if she stayed with them. The salt water carried away Atlanna's tears as she returned to Atlantis, leaving Tom to raise Arthur alone.

Arthur wasn't like the other kids. He swam like a fish—and talked with them too! While the other kids rode the waves on boogie boards, Arthur rode the backs of dolphins. When Tom found Arthur sitting on the ocean floor playing with a sea turtle, he knew without a doubt his son was special.

Other people noticed too, and some of them were cruel. Arthur's differences made him an outcast. When he got older and learned about Atlantis, he found out he was an outcast there too—the evil Atlantean king had declared it a crime for Atlanteans to have children with humans. Half-human and half-Atlantean, Arthur didn't know where he belonged.

Before she went away, Atlanna had predicted that Arthur would one day unite the kingdoms of land and sea. At first Arthur didn't want that kind of responsibility. He resented the "surface dwellers" who teased him and called him "Aquaman." And he hated Atlantis for taking his mother away. But Arthur had been born with more than super-human muscle and the power to talk to fish. He had a noble heart. He left Tom's lighthouse to save passing ships from pirates. He rescued sea life from greedy poachers' nets. It was the beginning of a journey that would one day lead to the throne of Atlantis. Arthur's parents had shown that human and Atlantean could come together in love. It was Arthur's destiny to prove it to the world.

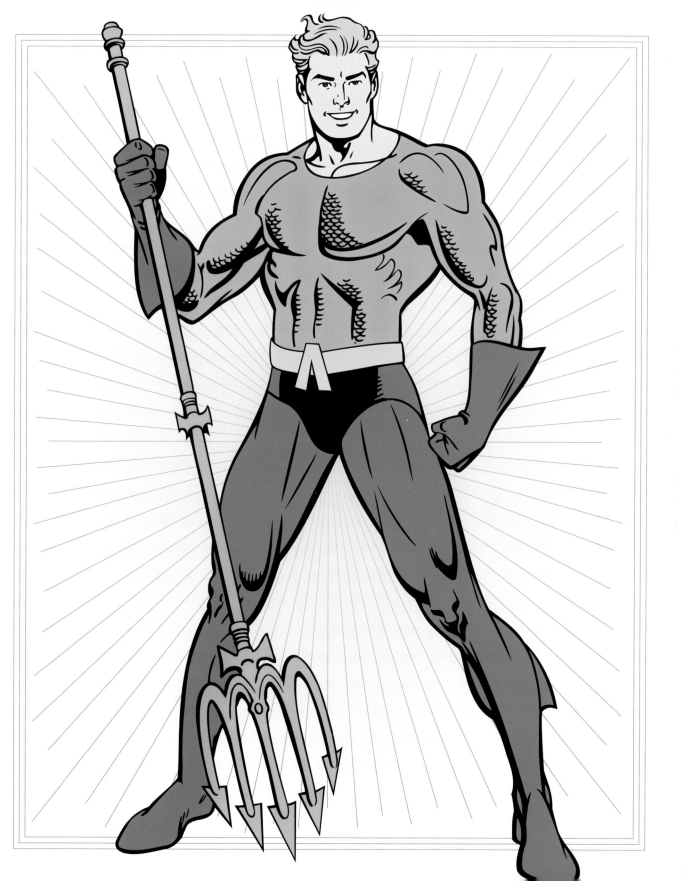

MERA

Princess Mera dreamed she'd meet a handsome king. Then she would defeat him and take over his kingdom.

Mera was the eldest daughter of King Ryus of Xebel. From an early age she trained to behave like a proper princess. In Xebel, that meant learning battle tactics and hand-to-hand combat. She also mastered hydrokinesis—the power to shape water with her mind. Mera was an excellent student. She was the strongest and swam the fastest. And her water powers were extraordinary—Mera could hold back a tidal wave!

King Ryus was a single father who raised Mera to have a heart full of hatred. He told stories about the terrible people of Atlantis. In truth, there was little difference between Xebel and Atlantis. They were all one people. But Ryus convinced Mera that Atlantis wanted to destroy Xebel. Mera believed him. She promised to defeat the Atlantean king. Surely he must be the most wicked of all.

Finally Mera was ready for her mission. King Ryus proclaimed that her reward would be to marry his army chief, Nereus. Mera did not want to marry Nereus. (Why would he even think that a husband was a reward, she wondered?) But she couldn't defy her father who had raised her on his own. King Ryus gave her a final gift—a necklace called the Shell of Sounds. It had belonged to Mera's mother and was said to contain a message. Filled with fury and determination, Mera set out to find the Atlantean king.

Her search led to the surface world. She met sailors who knew the Atlantean king as "Aquaman." They said he was a hero. Mera scoffed. It couldn't be true! But when she met Aquaman, he wasn't what she expected. He was rescuing stranded orca whales. She helped him with hydrokinesis. Aquaman was impressed. He invited Mera to lunch. This mission was not going as planned! The more they talked, the more Mera questioned everything she'd been taught. Aquaman was selfless and kind. He had no plan to attack Xebel. Mera felt torn between her duty to Xebel and the feelings in her heart.

She remembered her mother's necklace and rushed to the sea to listen to its message. Through the Shell of Sounds, her mother told her to trust herself. To marry whomever she wanted, or no one at all. To leave behind her father's demands and be free.

Mera found strength in her mother's words. She abandoned her mission to destroy and stayed with Aquaman as his partner, his equal, and someday the Queen of Atlantis.

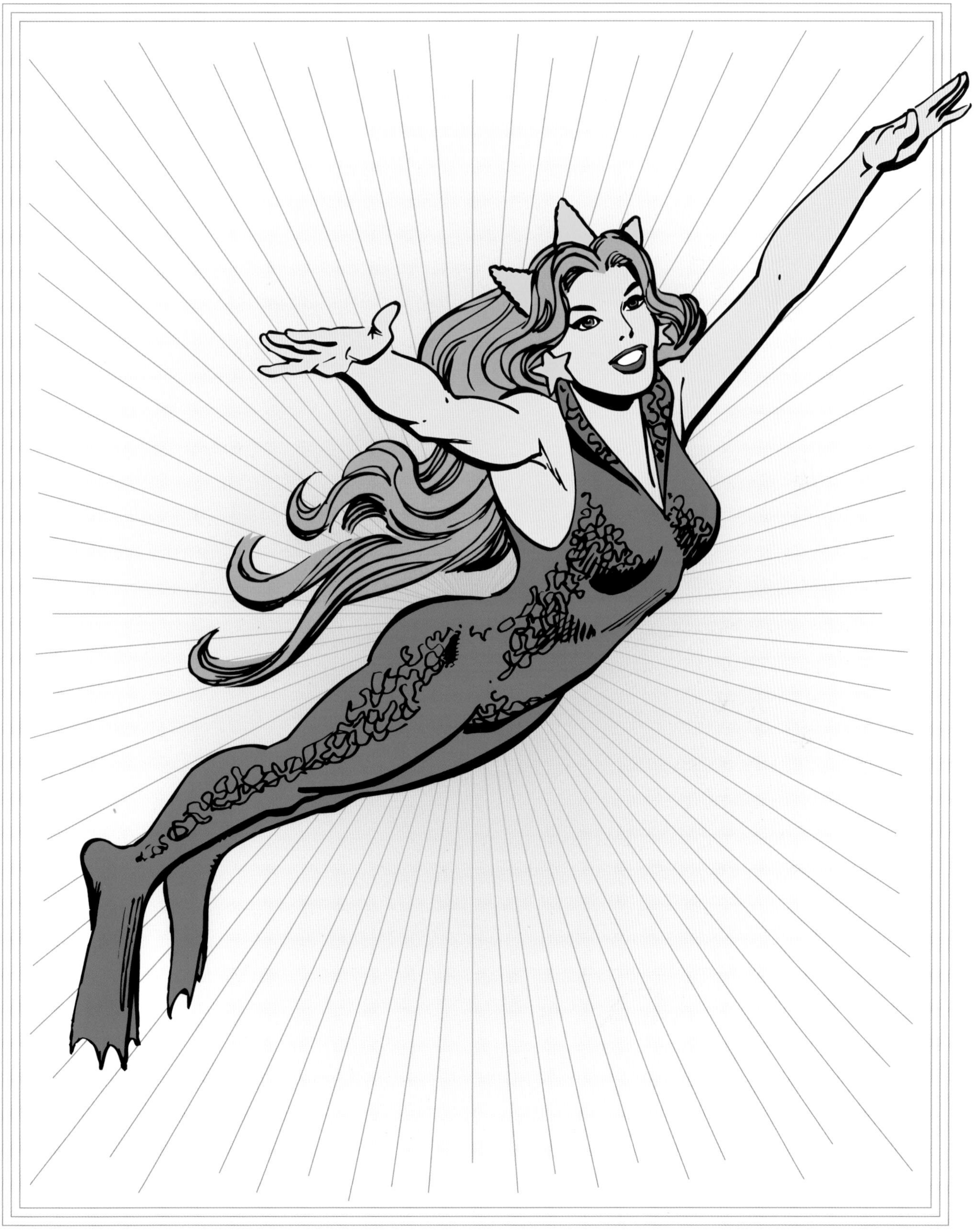

AQUALAD

Jackson Hyde was afraid of water. His parents always warned him that something terrible would happen if he touched so much as a drop. Growing up in the desert town of Silver City, New Mexico, it was easy to stay dry. Sometimes it was even a good thing—there's no fussing over bath time when you never have a bath. As Jackson got older he started to wonder about his parents' warnings. Was there something they weren't telling him? And what about the mysterious eel-like tattoos that snaked around both of his arms? Jackson couldn't remember getting them. Why would two overprotective parents cover their baby with tattoos but never explain why? There had to be more to the story.

So one day when he was a teenager, Jackson walked out into the rain. His whole life changed at the first drop of water on his skin. His tattoos glowed. His strength grew beyond human. The water even obeyed his commands! Jackson had the power of hydrokinesis—the ability to form water into shapes. He could change its temperature, turn it sharp as a sword, or even pull it out of the air and blast it like a fire hose! The boy who'd never taken a bath was now the world's most powerful showerhead! Jackson felt afraid but also wonderful, like a secret part of himself was finally set free. Why had his parents hidden the truth?

The reason was worse than anything Jackson had ever imagined. His birth father was the cruel Super-Villain known as Black Manta! Jackson's mother, an outcast Atlantean named Lucia, would do anything to keep him safe from his villainous dad. She'd hidden Jackson in the desert so that water would never trigger his powers and attract attention.

Now that Jackson knew the truth, he felt torn. He rejected his father's wicked ways. But living a false life felt wrong too. Lucia wanted him to hide anything that made him stand out. Finally, Jackson left home to find his own path in life. His choice meant that he'd someday come face to face with Black Manta. However, he would also find friends like the Teen Titans and teachers like Aquaman.

He didn't know it at the time, but the boy who was once afraid of water was on his way to becoming the king of the sea.

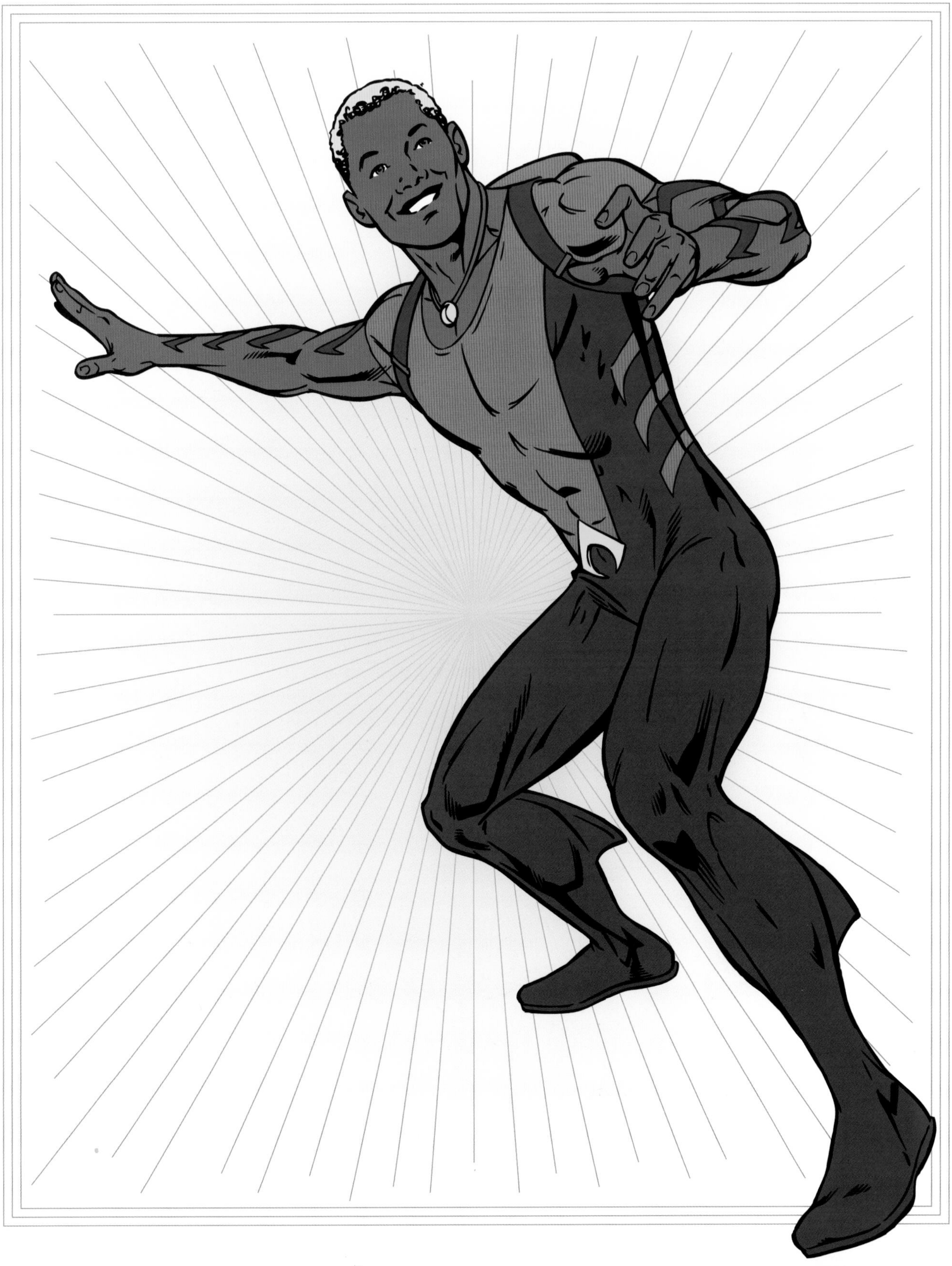

FIRESTORM

Ronnie Raymond was a football star at Bradley High School, though he was not the smartest kid in the class. Professor Martin Stein, on the other hand, was one of the most brilliant nuclear physicists on Earth. He had even won the Nobel Prize!

One night, some troublemakers tricked Ronnie into joining their scheme to blow up Professor Stein's nuclear fission lab experiment. (They planned to blame Ronnie for the crime.) But when they knocked out Professor Stein, Ronnie ran to his rescue.

It was too late. There was a big explosion—and it was so powerful, that Ronnie and Professor Stein were somehow fused into one body. This new body had a flaming head of hair and amazing superpowers. He called himself Firestorm, after the crackling flames on his head. Firestorm quickly flew off to capture the criminals who had caused the blast.

Although Ronnie and Professor Stein had two very different minds, Firestorm only had a single body. It's complicated. After the original fusing, Ronnie and the Professor recovered and were able to go their separate ways. But there was also this third superpowered being, Firestorm. And whenever his powers and intelligence were needed, Ronnie and Professor Stein found their way back to Firestorm. In this form, Ronnie would control what Firestorm says and does. It's hard to imagine, but Professor Stein lived as a voice in Firestorm's mind—offering expert advice to guide his actions. His training in nuclear physics made best use of Firestorm's powers. And when he wasn't directing Firestorm's actions, he was still a physics professor.

Sometimes called the Nuclear Man, Firestorm could fly, pass through walls, and shoot powerful blasts. Most amazing of all, he could transform the very matter of things around him, even creating objects out of thin air. This power didn't work on living things like plants, animals, or people. Since Ronnie was only a teenager at the time of the blast, Firestorm really needed the wise professor's guidance. When Firestorm joined the Justice League, the more experienced Super Heroes also had a lot to teach him about how to use his powers responsibly. Fortunately for Firestorm, he had many cool heads to show him the way.

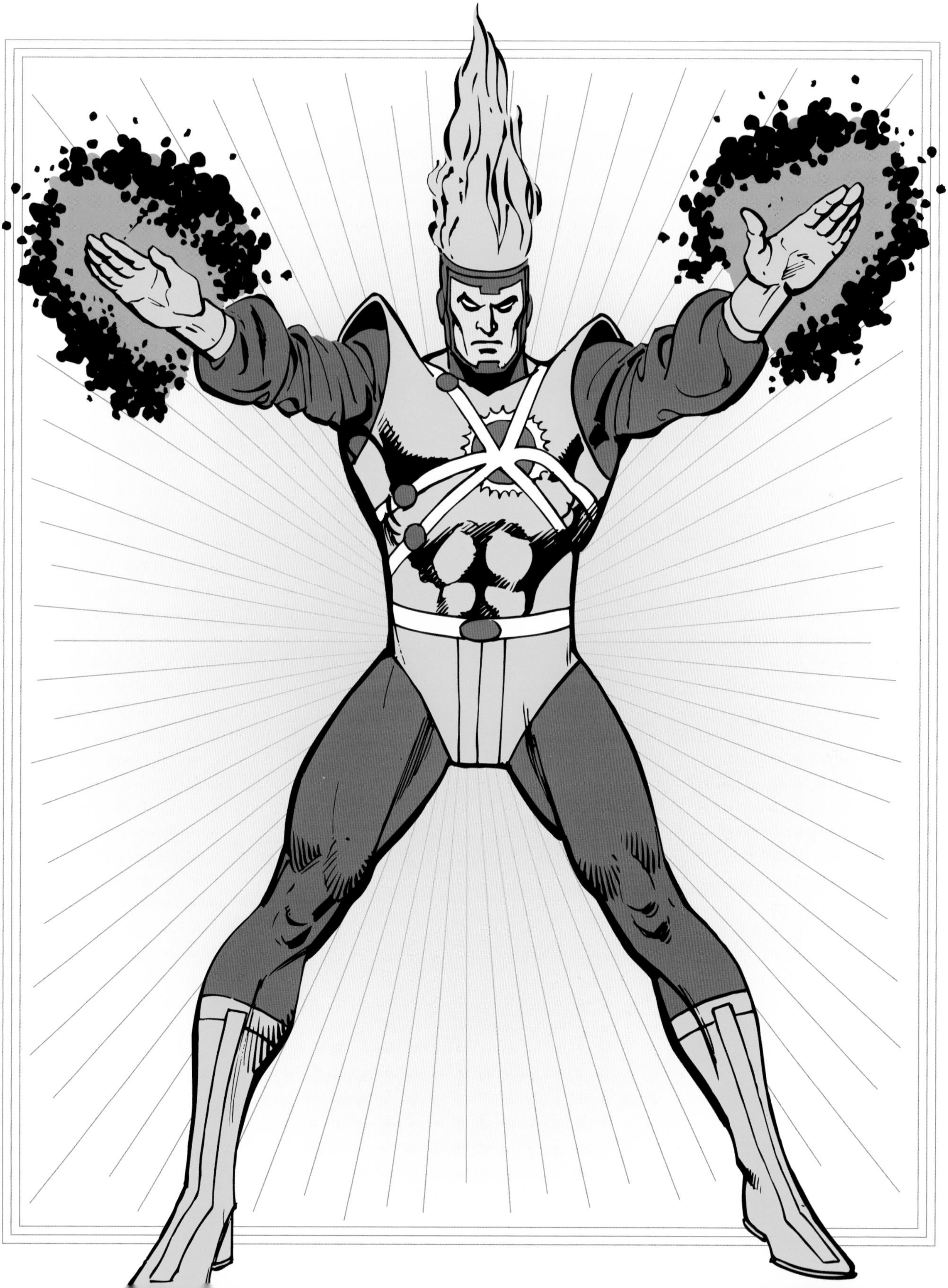

THE ATOM

Professor Ray Palmer was a brilliant physics teacher at Ivy University. When he found some matter from a white dwarf star that had fallen to Earth, he did what he always did. He experimented. He used some of the matter to make a special lens. He wanted to see if this lens could shrink things. He thought it would be pretty amazing if, say, you could shrink a car to fit in a shoebox, ship it somewhere, and then enlarge it to its regular size. When he wasn't teaching classes, he kept refining his technology.

One day while he was exploring a cave with some of his students, there was an avalanche. The opening to the cave was blocked by rocks that slid down the mountain. The group was trapped inside. Luckily, Ray had his shrinking lens with him. Though he had never experimented on a human before, he decided to try to shrink himself. It was risky—but it was the only way to save his students. He stepped away from the group, aimed his lens at his own body, and . . . it worked!

Once he was the size of a bug, he could easily squeeze through the cracks between the fallen rocks and clear away the rubble from the other side. Not only did he save the students, but he proved his shrinking machine could work on human beings. And, when the rescue operation was finished, Ray was able to return to his normal size.

With his new shrinking powers, Ray named himself The Atom, after the tiny particles that make up all matter. He designed a costume that would shrink and grow with him. The power to become microscopically tiny in the blink of an eye came in really handy. The Atom could hide and surprise criminals who wouldn't see him coming. He could slip through locks or into someone's pocket. His special technology enabled him to stay just as strong and heavy at one inch tall as he was at his full height.

Thanks to science, an impressive brain, and courage, the genius physicist transformed himself into a Super Hero.

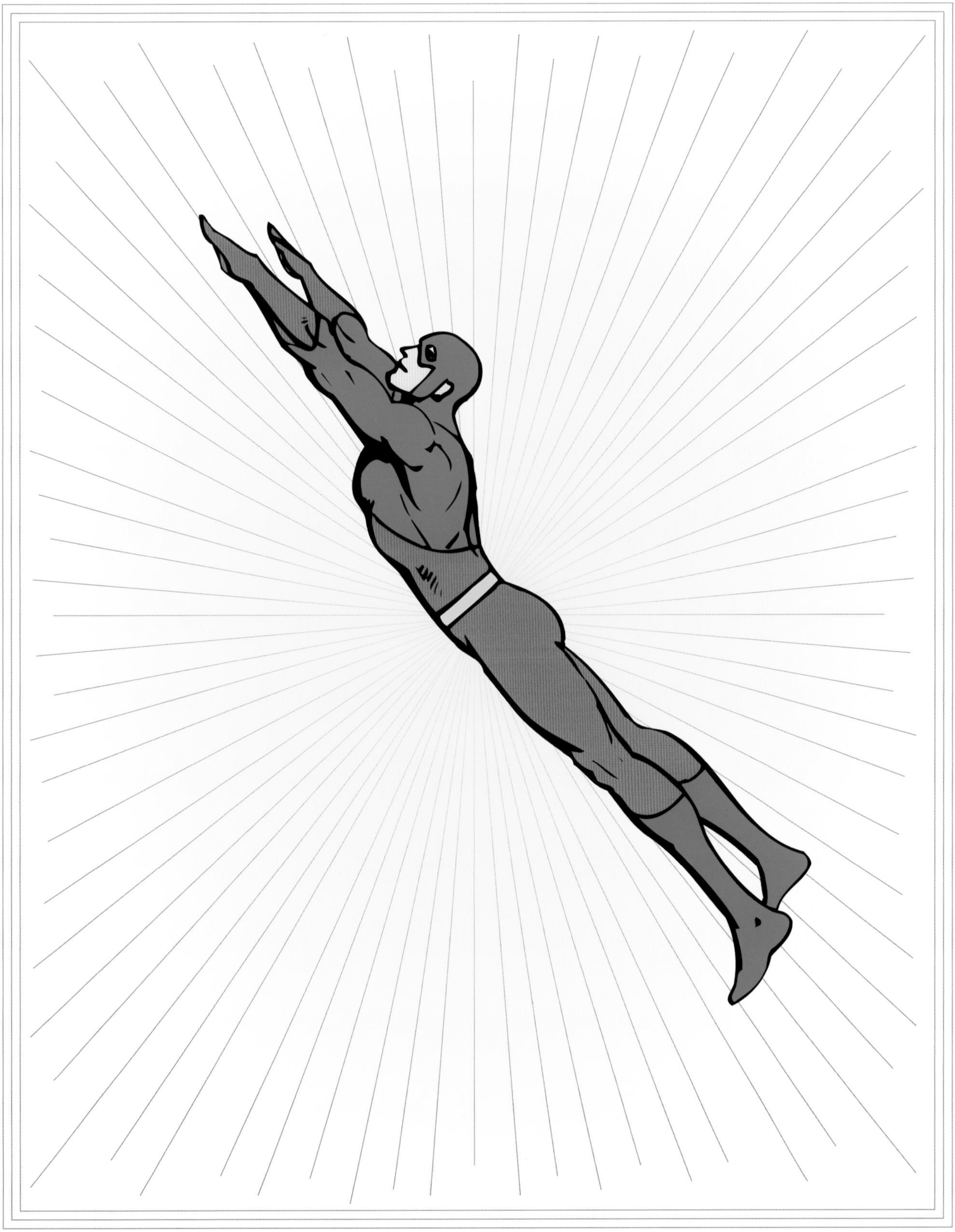

BLACK CANARY

Lots of kids think their parents are like superheroes. Dinah Lance's mother actually *was* one! A long, long time ago, Dinah's mom fought crime on the streets of Gotham City. Her name was Black Canary. Dinah always knew that when she grew up, she wanted to follow in her mother's footsteps.

With help from her mother and her Super Hero friends, Dinah learned all kinds of fighting techniques and detective skills. Hours of practice day after day, year after year, gave her great strength, agility, and expertise in martial arts. She also had a skill that nobody could teach her, a power her mother never had. Dinah had a thunderous Canary Cry. She was born with this amazing power to blast a sonic scream from her mouth. The sound of her voice was strong enough to punch through metal or stop a speeding car!

After years of training, Dinah's mother finally realized her daughter was ready to take over, and that she could step down. That's when Dinah became the new Black Canary. Roaring through the streets of the city on her high-tech motorcycle, Black Canary let the villains of the world know there was a new Super Hero in town. Soon she earned a reputation as an expert crime fighter. She fought Super-Villains as a member of the Justice League along with Superman, Batman, Wonder Woman and their friends. Later on, she teamed up with Batgirl and Huntress to form the girl-powered group known as Birds of Prey.

Throughout her crime-fighting career, Dinah paid it forward by helping train many younger Super Heroes, just as her mother trained her.

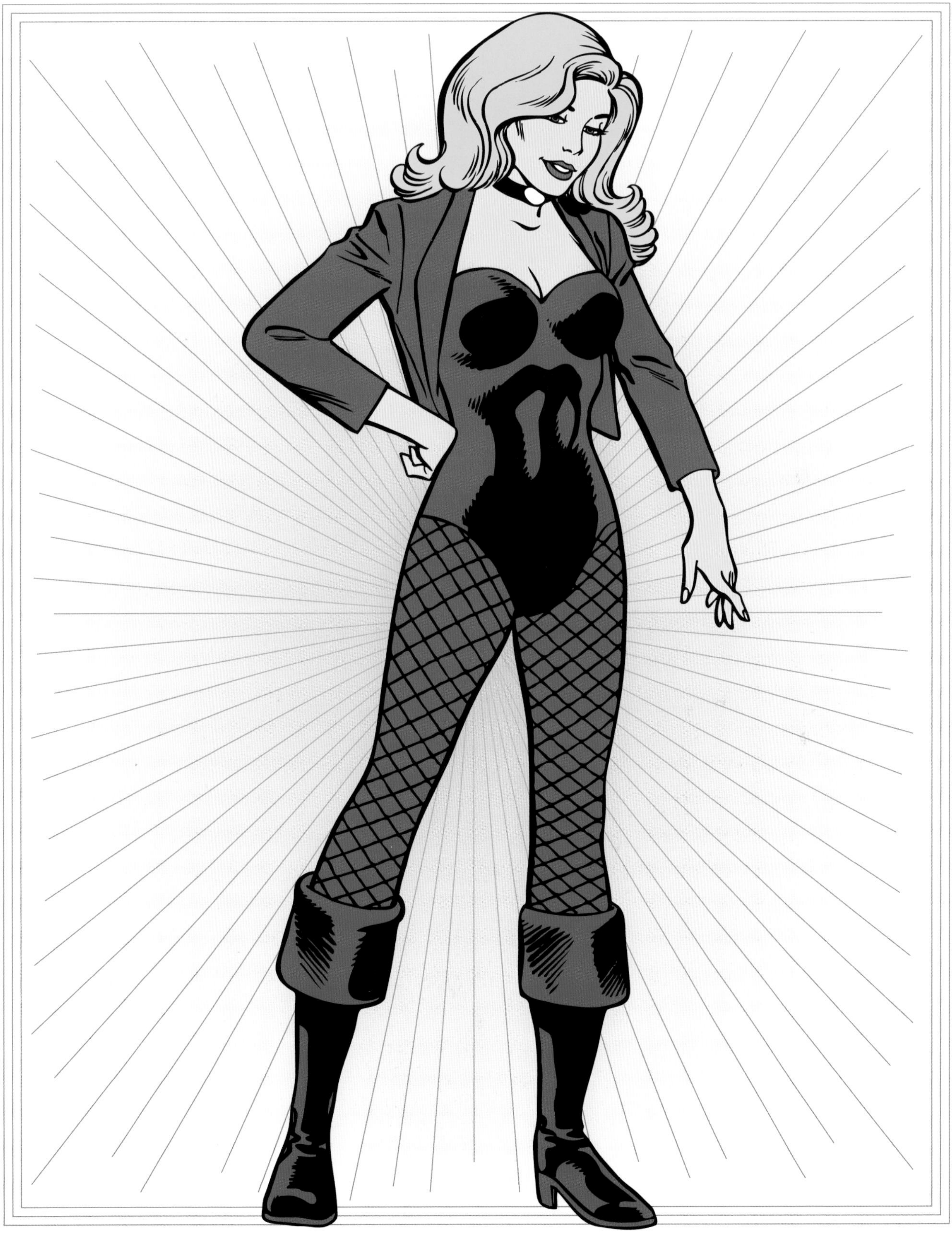

THE FLASH

"*Barry—you're always late! Why are you so slow?*" Iris West loved her fiancé Barry Allen, but he drove her crazy. He was never on time!

Barry hated to disappoint Iris, but sometimes he had to. He worked for the Central City Police Department as a scientist, solving crimes in a laboratory. When he was on a big case, everything else had to wait.

One night Barry worked late at the lab. He was standing in front of a cabinet full of chemicals when a bolt of lightning crashed through the window! It electrified Barry and spilled chemicals all over him. He was dizzy but somehow unhurt. He was also confused. The lightning had broken only certain jars, as if it had a mind of its own. Barry staggered out to the street. He had no idea how much his life had changed.

He just wanted to go home and into his bed. He spotted a taxi down the street—a stroke of luck at that late hour. Then the taxi quickly drove away. Barry ran after the car—and somehow passed it as if it was standing still! How was that possible? Maybe he was still woozy from the lightning? He stopped at a diner. A waitress passing by him dropped her tray. The food tumbled towards the floor, but to Barry, the French fries and napkins looked as if they were falling in slow motion. He scooped everything up and handed the tray to the astonished waitress. This was no dream—Barry had super-speed!

Off he ran! Up the sides of buildings! In circles so fast, he made a twister! He could even run on water—he moved so quickly that his body never sunk. Barry somehow knew just how to use his power. If he pushed himself to the limit, he could break the speed of light and move forward or backward through time. Everything about Barry was super-fast—his reflexes, his healing, even his thinking.

Barry's childhood hero had been a speedster called The Flash. Barry took that as his own Super Hero name. He designed a costume and a special ring to carry it in. Whenever he needed to suit up, he would press a button and be dressed and ready in *no* time!

With so many people to rescue and villains to catch, Barry was later than ever to meet his fiancée, Iris. She would never guess that slowpoke Barry Allen had become The Fastest Man Alive!

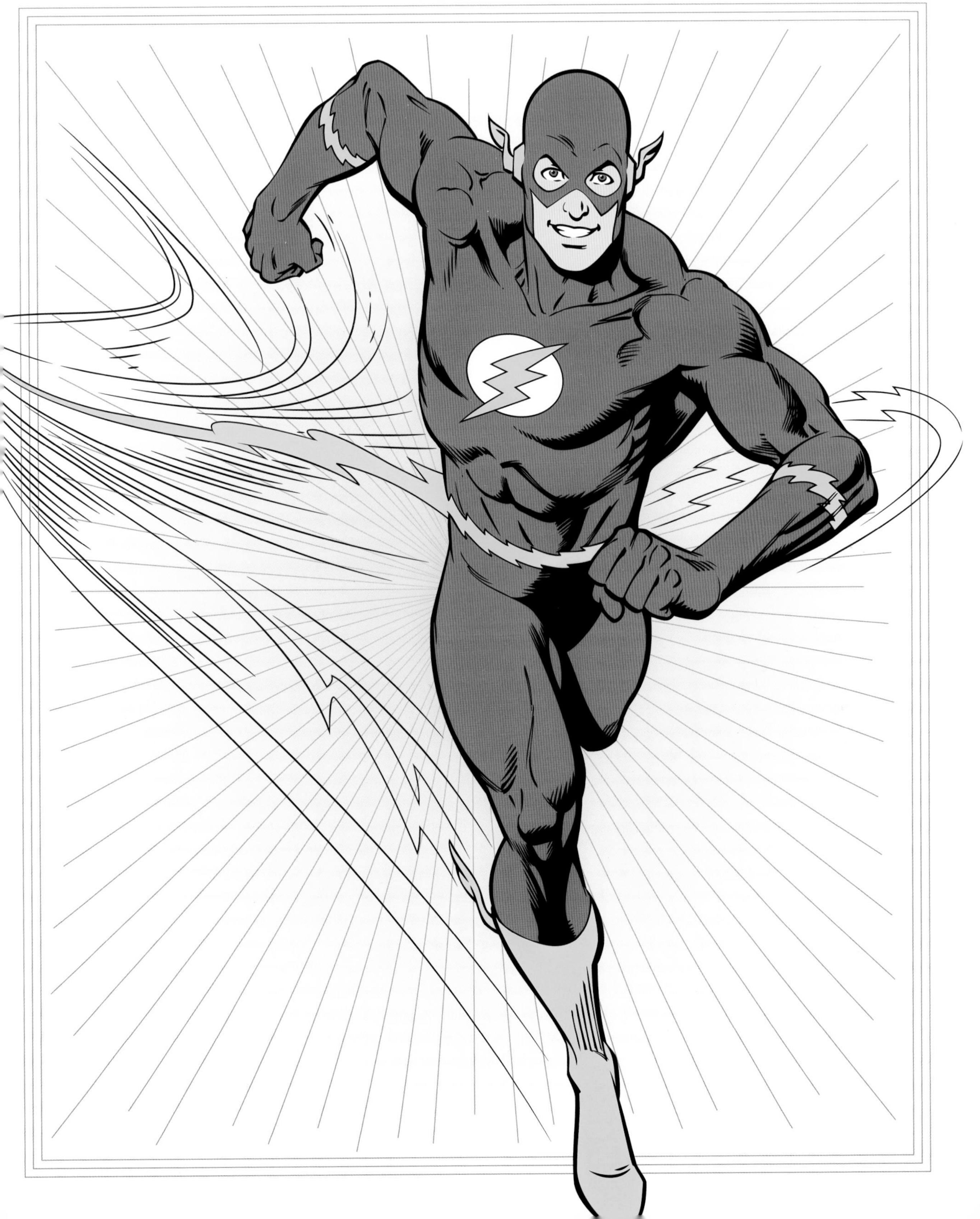

 GREEN LANTERN

HAL JORDAN

Hal Jordan was very brave and talented. And he knew it! He was the ace test pilot at the Ferris Aircraft Company. No airplane was too fast or too dangerous for him. He didn't mean to brag, but why hide it when you're the best there is? Hal thought he could accomplish anything he set his mind to.

Hal was alone at work when a mysterious green glow lifted him into the air! He landed in the desert next to a crashed spaceship. In the wreckage was a creature from another world. It was bald and red and wore a green uniform. Strangest of all, Hal could hear its thoughts.

The spaceman's name was Abin Sur. He knew he was badly hurt and wouldn't last long. He gave Hal a glowing green ring and told him that it was the most powerful tool in the universe. Its green energy could do anything Hal imagined—if his willpower was strong enough. Abin Sur had commanded the ring to bring him an honest and fearless human to replace him. The wounded spaceman gave Hal a power battery to charge the ring and told him to always fight against evil and injustice. Then he was gone.

The ring had chosen well. Hal's strong will used the ring to tremendous effect. With his first energy burst he picked up a mountaintop! He created energy blasts and force fields, testing his mysterious ring's powers. Earth had a powerful new hero.

There was more to being a Green Lantern than Hal understood right away. One day a beam carried him to a distant planet called Oa. Waiting there were the green rings' creators—the Guardians of the Universe. These wise old beings wanted to make sure that Abin Sur had chosen a worthy replacement. Hal found out there were thousands of peacekeepers just like him all over the universe. They were known as the Green Lantern Corps. When problems were too big for one Lantern to handle, they could count on each other for backup.

Seeing these brave warriors from the far reaches of the galaxy, Hal Jordan started to become humble. He wasn't the bravest or the best. Sometimes he would call for help. And he could trust that there were thousands of heroes willing to answer the call. Heroes of every size and shape, united in their love of justice and in their devotion to the Green Lantern oath:

In brightest day, in blackest night, no evil shall escape my sight.
Let those who worship evil's might, beware my power, Green Lantern's light.

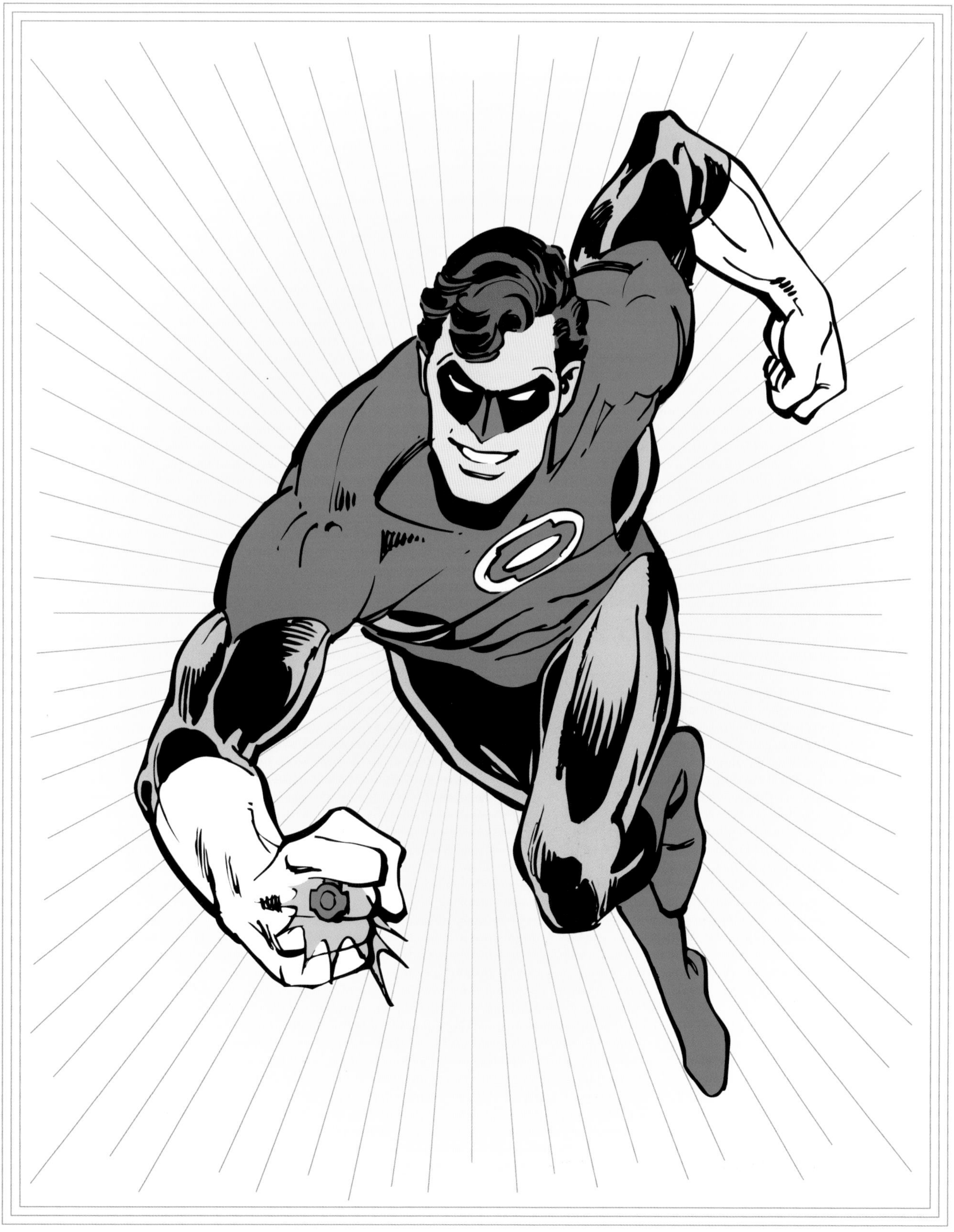

GREEN LANTERN

JOHN STEWART

Visitors to a certain candy store in downtown Detroit couldn't believe their eyes. Between boxes of chocolates at the soda counter sat an unlikely pair—Hal Jordan (better known as the intergalactic peacekeeper, Green Lantern) and an unemployed architect named John Stewart. Nobody would have guessed that Hal had come to Detroit to offer John a job as a Green Lantern—especially John.

John had woken up that day feeling frustrated. His mother, a community organizer, had raised him to speak out when he saw injustice. Sadly, he saw it everywhere. He wanted to make a difference in his poor neighborhood, but he was struggling to find work. When John saw a white police officer bully two innocent Black teens who were peacefully playing dominoes, he knew he had to speak up. He calmly, firmly convinced the officer to back down. He didn't know that Hal Jordan was watching.

The Guardians of the Universe had sent Hal to find John. Earth needed a backup Green Lantern, and the Guardians thought John was the right person for the job. Hal explained the situation. He described a dream job to John. John could have a chance to make the world fair and safe for all. And he would have the power of the ring and the Green Lantern Corps behind him. Of course John accepted!

John showed great skill right away. He had been a U.S. Marine, so he understood hard training and dangerous missions. Flying came to him quite naturally. And his work as an architect turned out to be the best preparation for using green light energy to make constructs. John's constructs—shields and buildings and vehicles—were creative and very well-made.

For his first mission, John had to help Hal protect a man who was running for president. The candidate, Senator Clutcher, said that someone was threatening him. John heard the senator speak and knew he was a racist. He was trying to get elected by turning white Americans against Black Americans. Although John had been brought on to help Hal with the mission, John couldn't bring himself to follow Hal's directions. He knew something was wrong. In the nick of time, John was able to prove that the senator had faked threats against himself in order to create racial hatred.

It was quickly clear why the Green Lantern Corps had chosen John. John's willingness to stand up to powerful people—and to speak up for what's right— would made him a great Green Lantern.

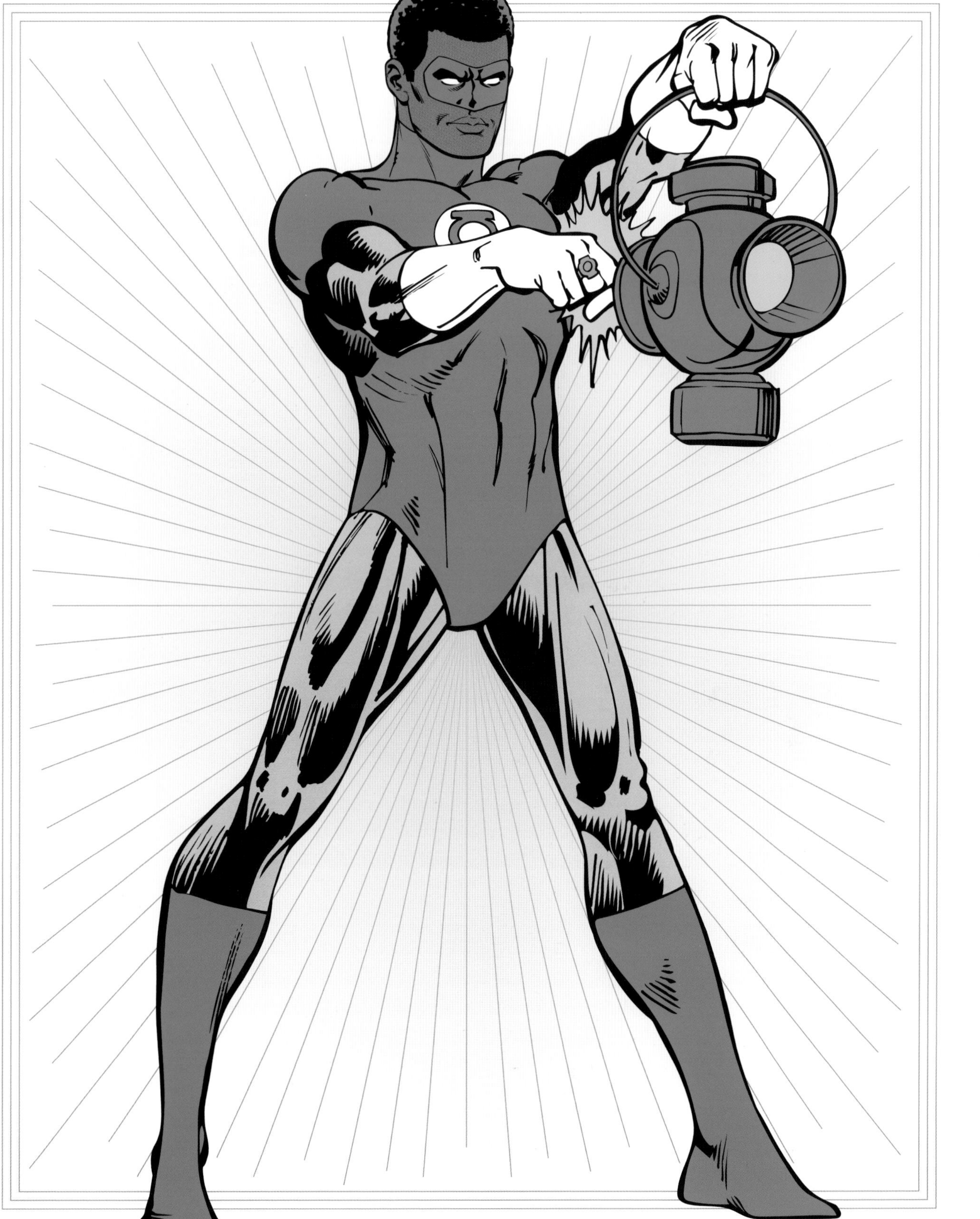

GREEN LANTERN

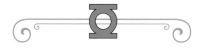

JESSICA CRUZ

Jessica Cruz hadn't left her apartment in four years. The thought of setting foot outside her door terrified her.

Jessica had once been bold and adventurous. Then she was the victim of a crime. Afterward she seemed fine. But she couldn't stop thinking about the shock of the crime, how she had been caught by surprise. Her anxiety grew until it was out of control. Eventually Jessica locked herself away from the world. Then her life changed in a flash of green light.

The Ring of Volthoom was different from other power rings. It was an ancient, evil thing with a mind of its own. It fed on fear. Its old wearer had been defeated and now it was looking for a new host. Jessica was the most frightened person it could find.

The ring flew into Jessica's apartment and attached itself to her hand. Jessica pulled but it wouldn't come off. The ring gave her all the powers of a Green Lantern—shields, flight, any energy construct she could imagine—but at a terrible price. The ring took over Jessica's body. It called her a puppet. Jessica felt helpless to stop it.

Super Heroes came to stop her. She battled the Justice League. She battled the Doom Patrol. Finally, Batman swooped in. He didn't try to fight Jessica. He talked to her instead. He told her that he, too, had been the victim of a crime. He said that people become heroes when they face their greatest fear. Jessica aimed her ring at Batman. Then she hesitated.

The ring screamed at Jessica to ignore Batman's words. It ordered her to blast him. Instead Jessica resisted. Batman had reminded her of the strong, confident person she used to be. She fought back against the ring. It was the hardest thing she'd ever done, but in the end Jessica won. She reclaimed control of her body. The ring's power was now hers to command.

Jessica accepted an offer to join the Justice League. As long as she wore the Ring of Volthoom, her life would be a struggle. But she didn't need to hide anymore. Jessica had learned that her courage was stronger than her fear.

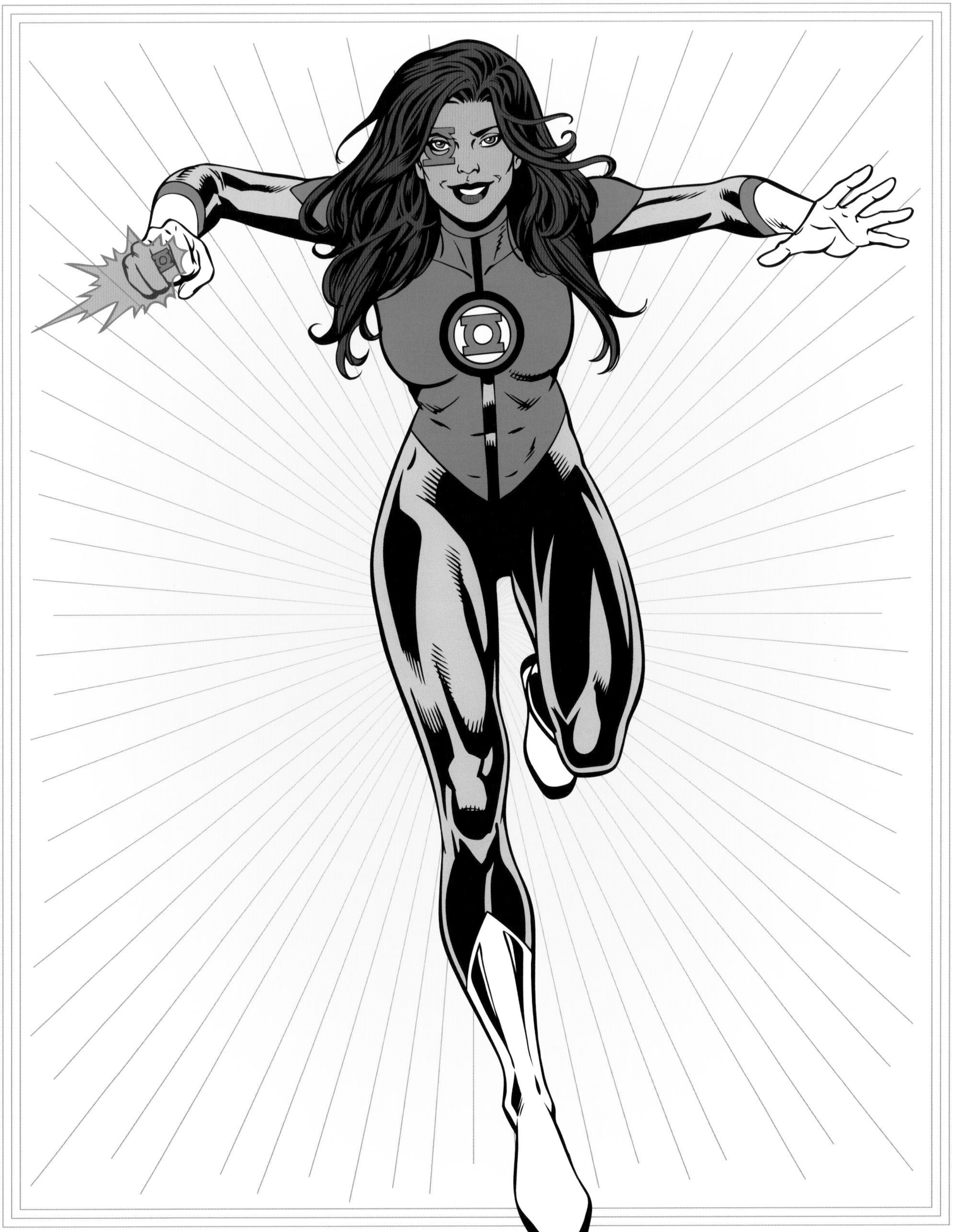

HAWKMAN & HAWKWOMAN

When the shape-shifting alien villain Byth went on the run, the police force of the planet Thanagar sent its two greatest officers to capture him. Shayera Hol and her husband, Katar, would follow him to the end of their star system if needed. And it was! Luckily, Thanagarian police have plenty of tools and technology to help them. First off, they wear large, feathered wings that enable them to fly far and fast. They also wear helmets that resemble the heads of Earth hawks. Sure enough, the Hols tracked Blyth with hawklike skill to the third planet in a distant star system, a planet called Earth.

The Hols had more high-tech tools to help them in their hunt. They used their spaceship's Absorbascon computer to learn everything they could about Earth and began their search. Working together, they caught Byth and returned him to Thanagarian prison.

Their brief visit to Earth left them interested in learning more about this curious planet. They decided to return there and study the human approach to law and order. This was the beginning of their new careers as Super Heroes.

Shayera chose to call herself Hawkwoman and Katar became Hawkman. They assumed secret identities as human museum directors named Shiera and Carter Hall. With help from the Absorbascon, they became experts in Earth history. They even studied ancient weapons. They both learned how to wield a mace—a spiked ball on a poll that they could swing with tremendous power and keen aim.

The two Hawks joined the Justice League, which was known for welcoming aliens including Superman and Martian Manhunter. People from faraway places made the group diverse, each bringing their own cool tools and technology. They showed the other members how the special Nth Metal from their planet is used to heal wounds. Worn in their belts, Nth Metal enabled Hawkman and Hawkwoman to survive all types of atmospheres—from the far reaches of the galaxy to deep down in the ocean. The Hawks were also able to communicate with birds. Super-strength and heightened senses rounded out the superpowers that made them special and important members of the team.

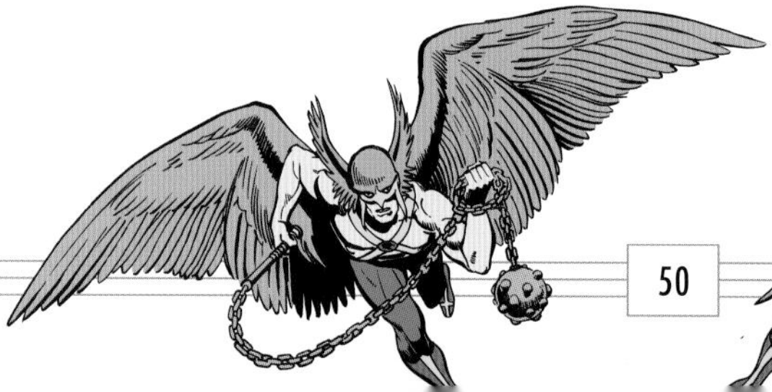

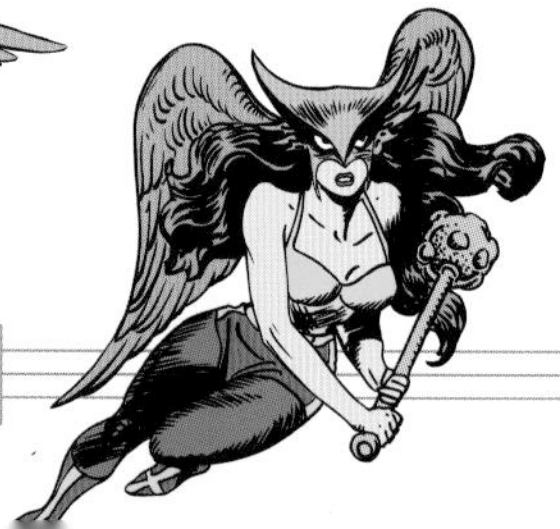

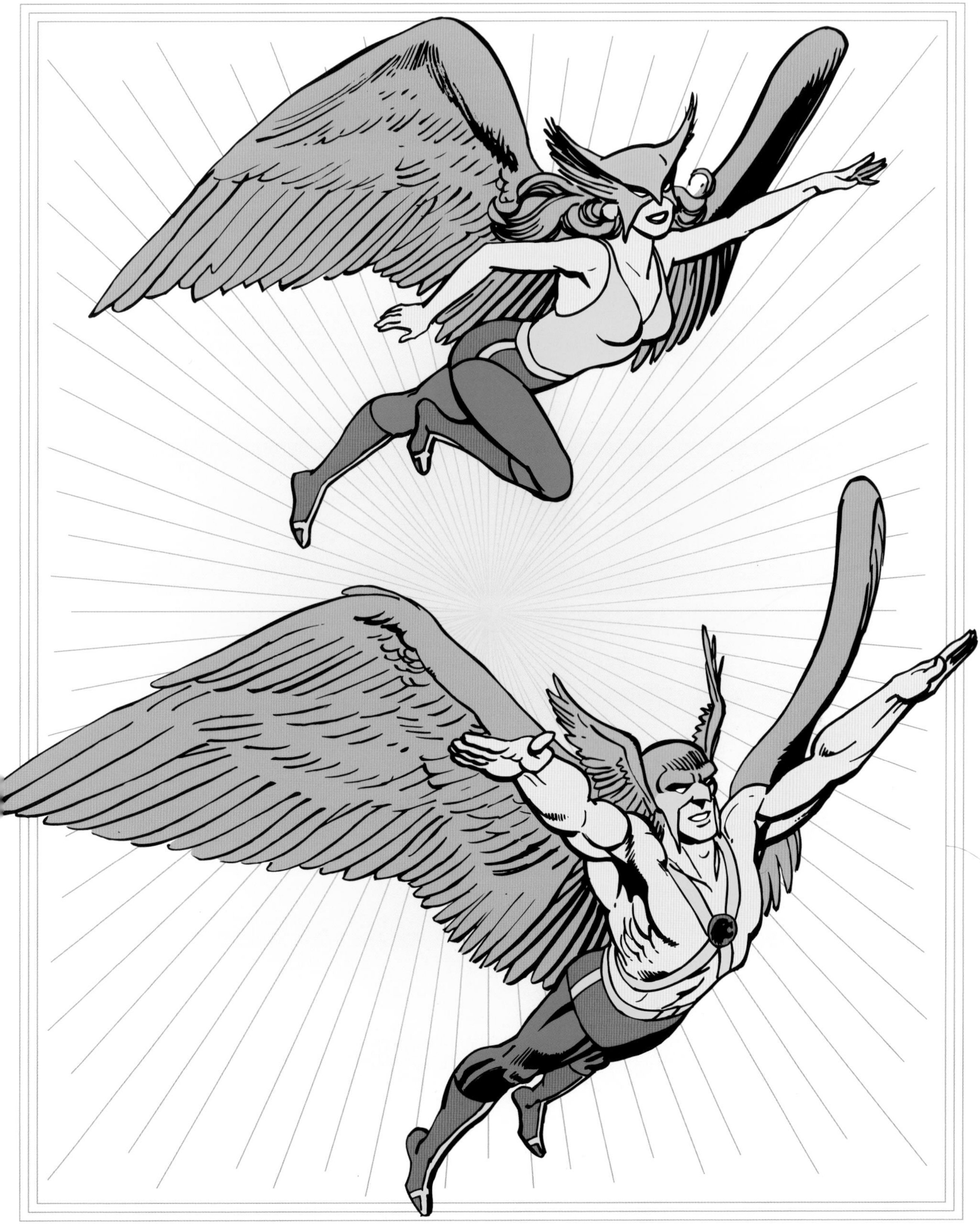

GREEN ARROW

Oliver Queen was a spoiled brat. His parents were rich, and Oliver thought that made him better than everyone else. He wore the trendiest clothes. He threw the wildest parties. He had the snobbiest friends. Oliver had every privilege in the world, and he took it all for granted.

One night Oliver was partying at sea on his luxury yacht. He treated the ship's crew poorly. He stayed up way too late. By the time he stumbled off to bed, Oliver could barely see where he was going. It's not so surprising he took a misstep and fell into the water. No one heard his cries for help—or if they did, they pretended not to. Oliver was lost at sea.

Oliver swam and swam. Just as he was about to give up hope, an island came into view. Oliver's excitement didn't last long—the island was deserted. Oliver's money meant nothing there. He would have to survive on his wits alone. He made himself a bow and arrows and learned to hunt for food. He fashioned a green suit out of plants so he could sneak about unseen. He learned how to make trick arrows using whatever was at hand, like the elastic from his socks. Oliver had discovered talents and strength he never knew he had. Months on this lonely island turned into years, and Oliver grew into the world's greatest archer.

At long last Oliver spotted a cargo ship near the island. He waved and shouted but it sailed right past. Oliver couldn't miss this chance to escape. He dove into the sea and swam to the ship.

An unpleasant surprise awaited Oliver when he climbed aboard—the ship had been taken over by pirates! Oliver used his incredible archery skills to defeat the pirates and save the crew. Oliver was a hero!

Home at last, Oliver let everyone think he was the shallow son of a billionaire as he was before. But he began a secret life as the Super Hero Green Arrow. His years on the island had taught him far more than how to use a bow. He now felt a bond with those who faced hunger and hopelessness. Oliver Queen had become a champion of the weak and the voiceless.

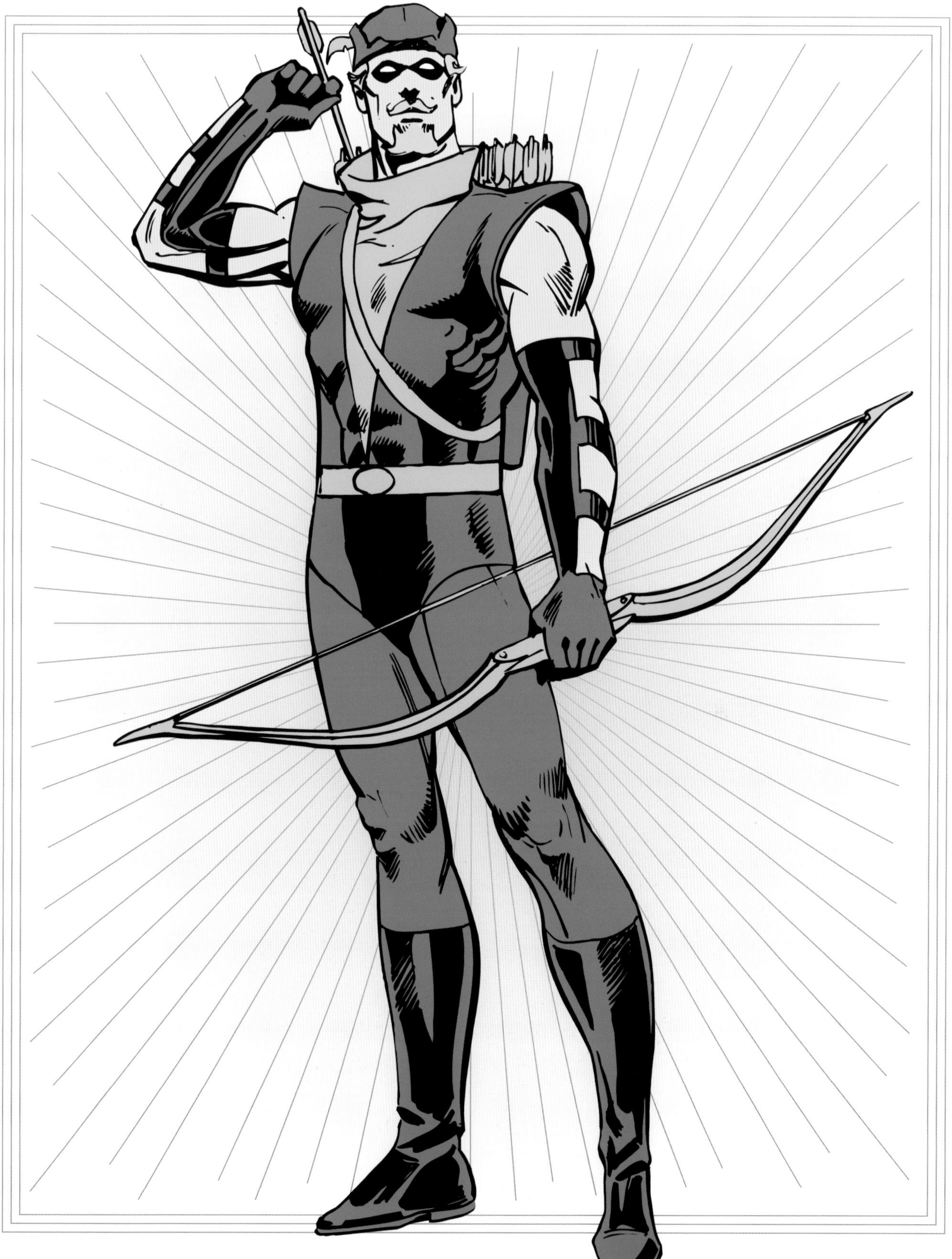

ZATANNA

Zatanna is a *magi*. Though she looks like a regular person, she, and other magi like her, use the power of magic in strange and powerful ways. Zatanna is one of the greatest magi on Earth.

She is a descendant of the great artist and inventor Leonardo Da Vinci. Her mother was the mysterious sorceress Sindella, and her father was Giovanni Zatara, who traveled around the world performing stage magic for audiences. Offstage, he would secretly use his magic to fight crime and break magical spells cast against the Earth by evil magi.

When Zatanna's father went missing one day, she set out to find him. On her quest, she met the Justice League. With help from Batman and Atom, she was able to find her father—trapped in another dimension. And together they rescued him. On this difficult mission, Zatanna had proven she was as great a hero as her father, and soon she joined the Justice League herself. Her magical gifts brought a new level of power to the team.

Zatanna casts her spells by speaking words backwards. If she said "erif wolb tuo" a raging fire would blow out like a birthday candle. If she said "nwod llaf," the villain she was up against would fall to the ground. Those spell-casting powers came in handy! She continued to perform magic tricks for adoring audiences. Whenever her Super Hero friends need a hand, Zatanna magically appears.

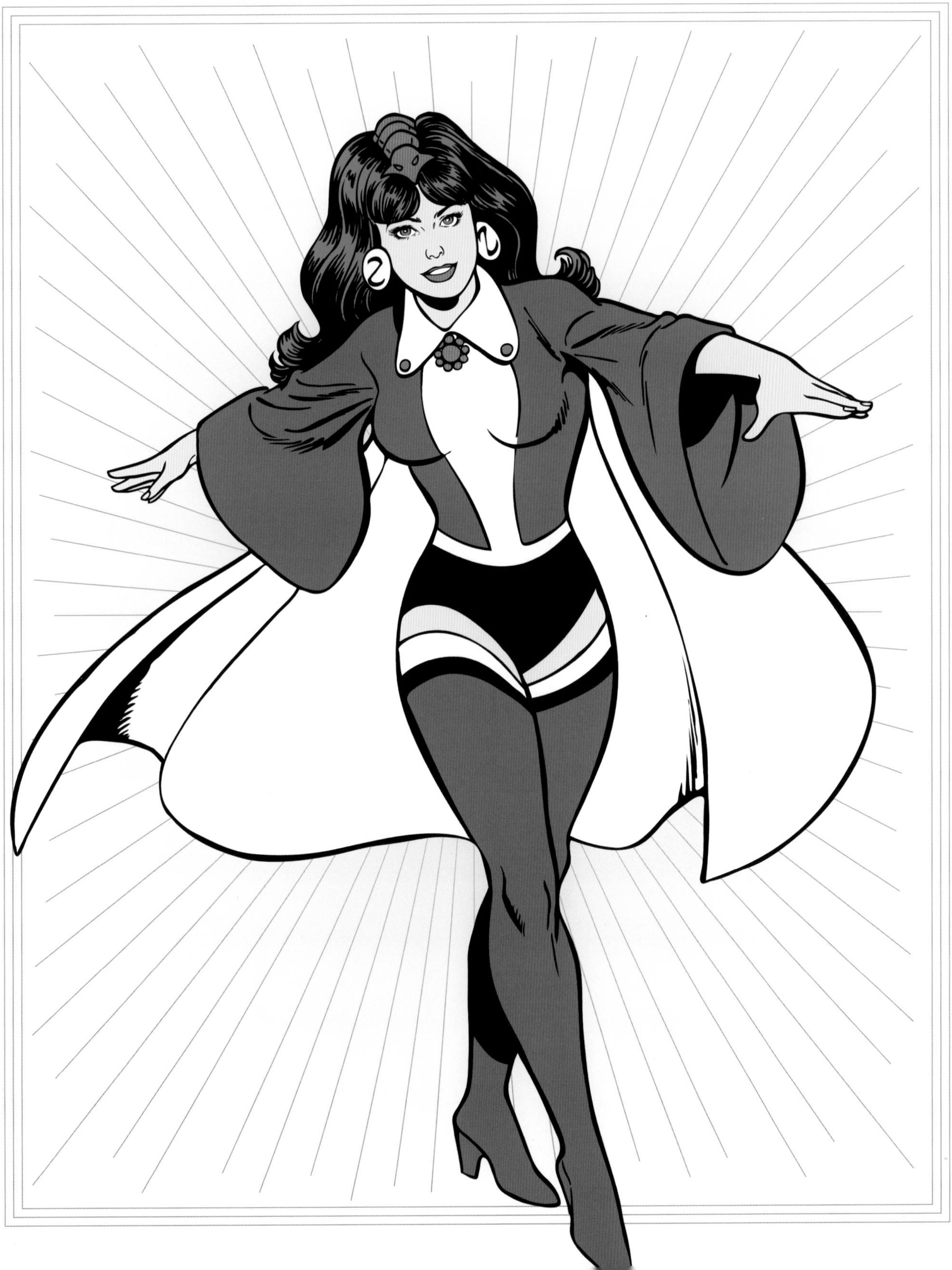

MARTIAN MANHUNTER

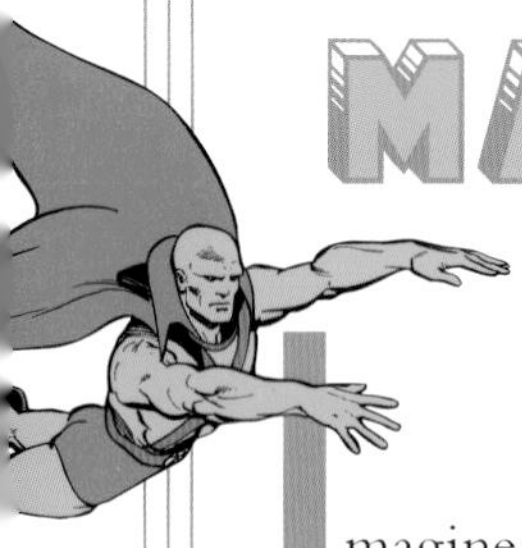

Imagine a world where nobody grows old and nobody feels lonely. Picture a society dedicated to justice and peace. Envision a place where people move things with their minds, and their bodies can shift into any shape. Now imagine watching that glorious world crumble before your eyes. That is the story of J'onn J'onzz, the Martian Manhunter.

Long ago on the planet Mars, J'onn J'onzz was a happy family man living with his wife M'yri'ah and their daughter K'hym. His job—Manhunter (the Martian word for police officer)—sounded exciting, but it really wasn't. Most Green Martians obeyed the law. They had learned their lessons from a violent past. They read each other's minds and shared each other's feelings. This ability connected them to one another in a unique and powerful way.

Then something terrible happened. A virus began to infect the Martians. It spread from person to person when they shared thoughts. The Martians struggled to stop using their mind powers. (It would be like asking humans to not speak a word to one another.) Only J'onn was able to resist and contain his thoughts. The rest of the Green Martians were destroyed. As the virus raged, J'onn found himself completely alone.

He wandered the Martian desert for years, until one day, a beam from the sky carried him to Earth. A human scientist named Dr. Erdel had accidentally brought him to Middleton, Colorado. Dr. Erdel had hoped to contact an extraterrestrial. Now he had one on his lawn. J'onn's sadness over the loss of his world remained overwhelming. Dr. Erdel didn't know how to help his strange visitor. To a human, J'onn's powers seemed miraculous. He could shape-shift, or make himself invisible. He was super-strong, could fly, and could even pass through walls like a ghost. He seemed capable of anything—except healing his own pain.

Dr. Erdel told J'onn that with all his powers, he could be a great champion on Earth. He could even be a Manhunter again—on a planet that really needed one. J'onn accepted this new challenge, and helping others gave him a reason to go on. J'onn would still grieve the Martians he loved and the world he lost. But he would find new friends in the Justice League, and he would use his powers to make his new home as peaceful and magnificent as his old one.

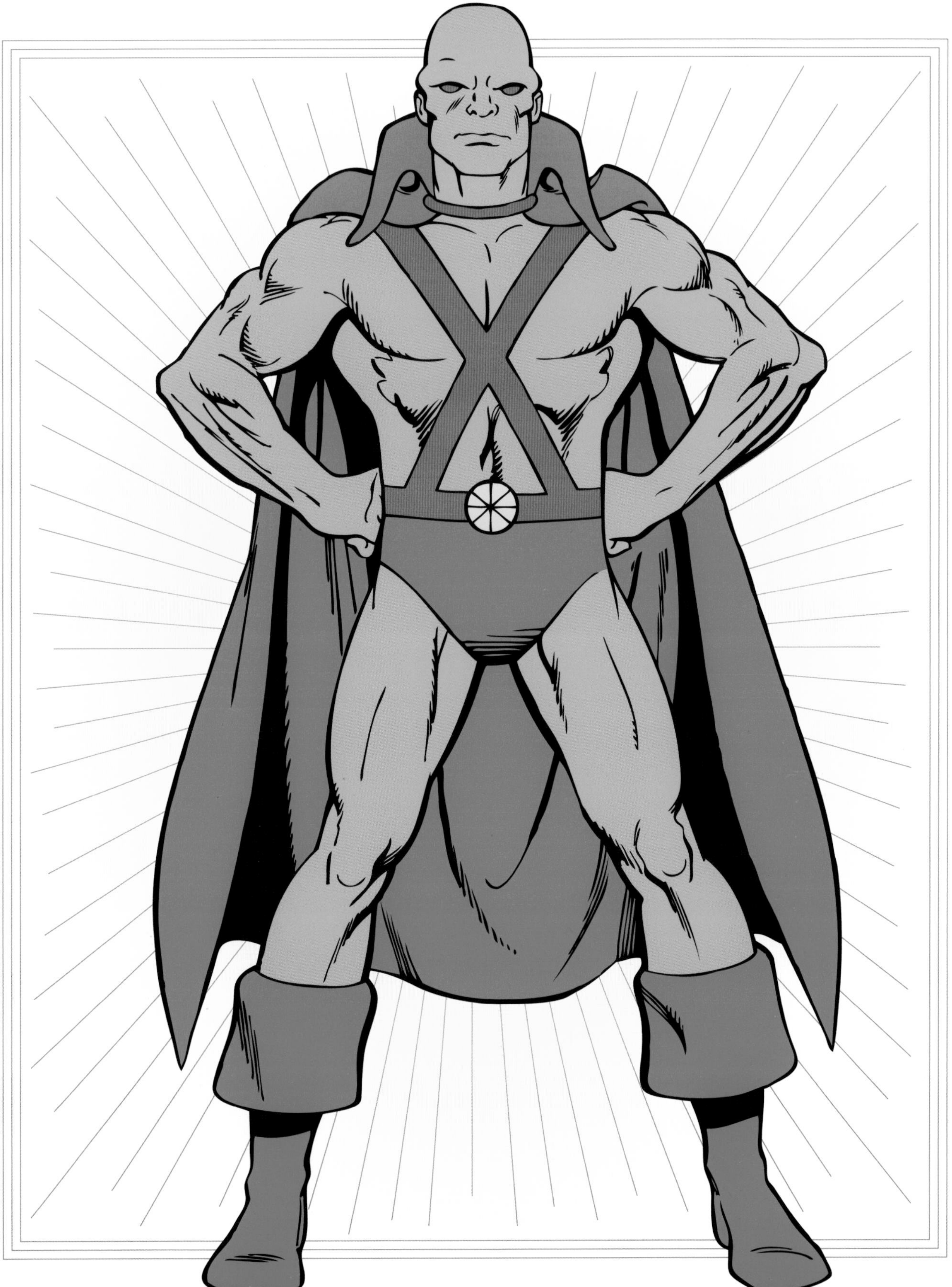

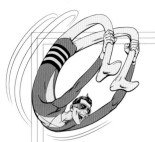

PLASTIC MAN

Some people think of Plastic Man as the Justice League's jester. Few realize that this comedian's career began on the wrong side of the law.

Patrick "Eel" O'Brian wasn't born bad. Orphaned at the age of 10, he tried to work hard and live honestly. But too many run-ins with bullies and gangsters wore him down. He fell in with a bunch of burglars called the Skizzle Shanks gang.

One night the gang robbed the Crawford Chemical Works. Eel was emptying the safe when a night watchman burst in. The gang made a run for it. Everyone got away except Eel. He stumbled into a barrel full of chemicals and got soaked from head to foot. He made it to the street just in time to watch his buddies speed away without him.

The police were on the way. Eel needed to flee but he was wounded and feeling sicker by the second. He ran until he reached the mountains outside the city. There he fainted on a rocky hiking trail. It looked like the end for Eel.

Eel awoke in a soft bed at Rest-Haven, a mysterious mountain monastery. Gentle monks nursed him back to health. They hid him from the police who had trailed him from the bungled burglary. Eel couldn't understand why the monks would help him. They knew he was a bad guy. A monk explained to Eel that he deserved a second chance.

Eel had been treated poorly his whole life. The monks' kindness changed something inside him. The goodness that had been there all along finally awoke. He was never a bad person. He had simply made some bad choices.

Eel was ready to get out of bed and start his new life. He stretched his arms—and they kept on stretching! The chemical spill had made his whole body like rubber!
He could bounce like a ball. He could make himself paper-thin or skyscraper-tall. A lamp, a ladder, an umbrella—Eel could stretch and twist his body into any shape at all.

He knew just what to do with his new superpower—he would make the most of his second chance. He would make smart choices and help bring out the goodness in others around him. A rough childhood had made Eel O'Brian a crook, but kindness made him Plastic Man!

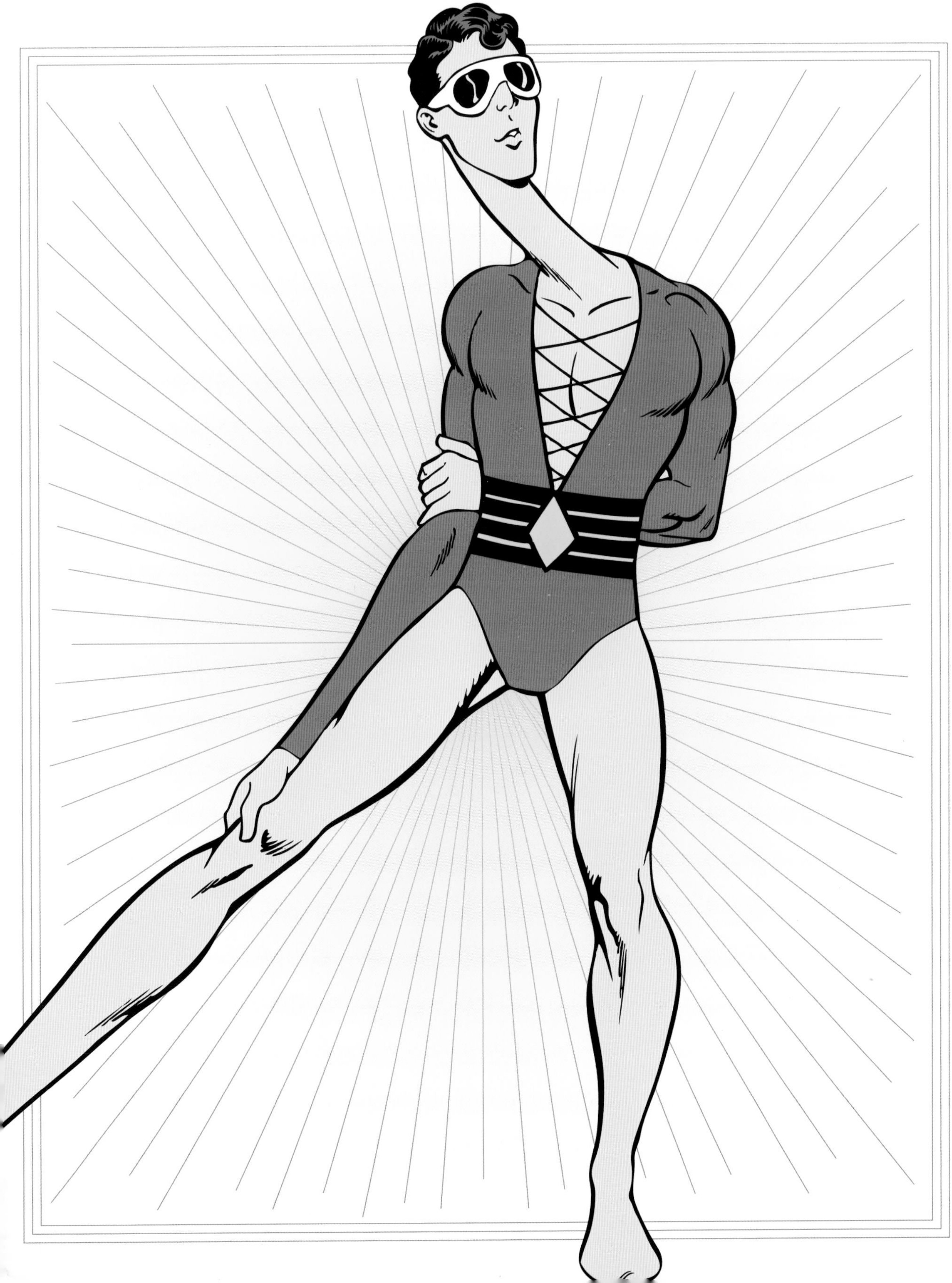

SHAZAM!

Billy Batson lost his parents when he was little and spent most of his childhood in foster homes. When he was young, he just wanted a *real* family. By the time he was 14, he wished he was a grown-up already so that he wouldn't need anyone to take care of him. Then one night, his wish sort of came true.

That night, he was transported to the Rock of Eternity, the secret fortress of the mighty wizard Shazam. Shazam explained to Billy that he had been protecting the realm for 3,000 years and that he had become too old to continue. He summoned Billy because he needed to find a replacement, and he knew that Billy had a pure heart.

The wizard described his special powers to Billy, which were granted to him by the gods: the wisdom of Solomon, the strength of Hercules, the stamina of Atlas, the power of Zeus, the courage of Achilles, and the speed of Mercury.

The old wizard demonstrated for Billy how he would shout "Shazam!" to transform into a powerful Super Hero. He instructed Billy to try, and the moment Billy shouted "Shazam!" he turned into a big, strong Super Hero as well. And as he did, the wizard's fortress began to crumble.

Though Billy would remain a teenager for much of the time, he now held the power to become not only a fully independent adult but a Super Hero whenever he wanted or needed to.

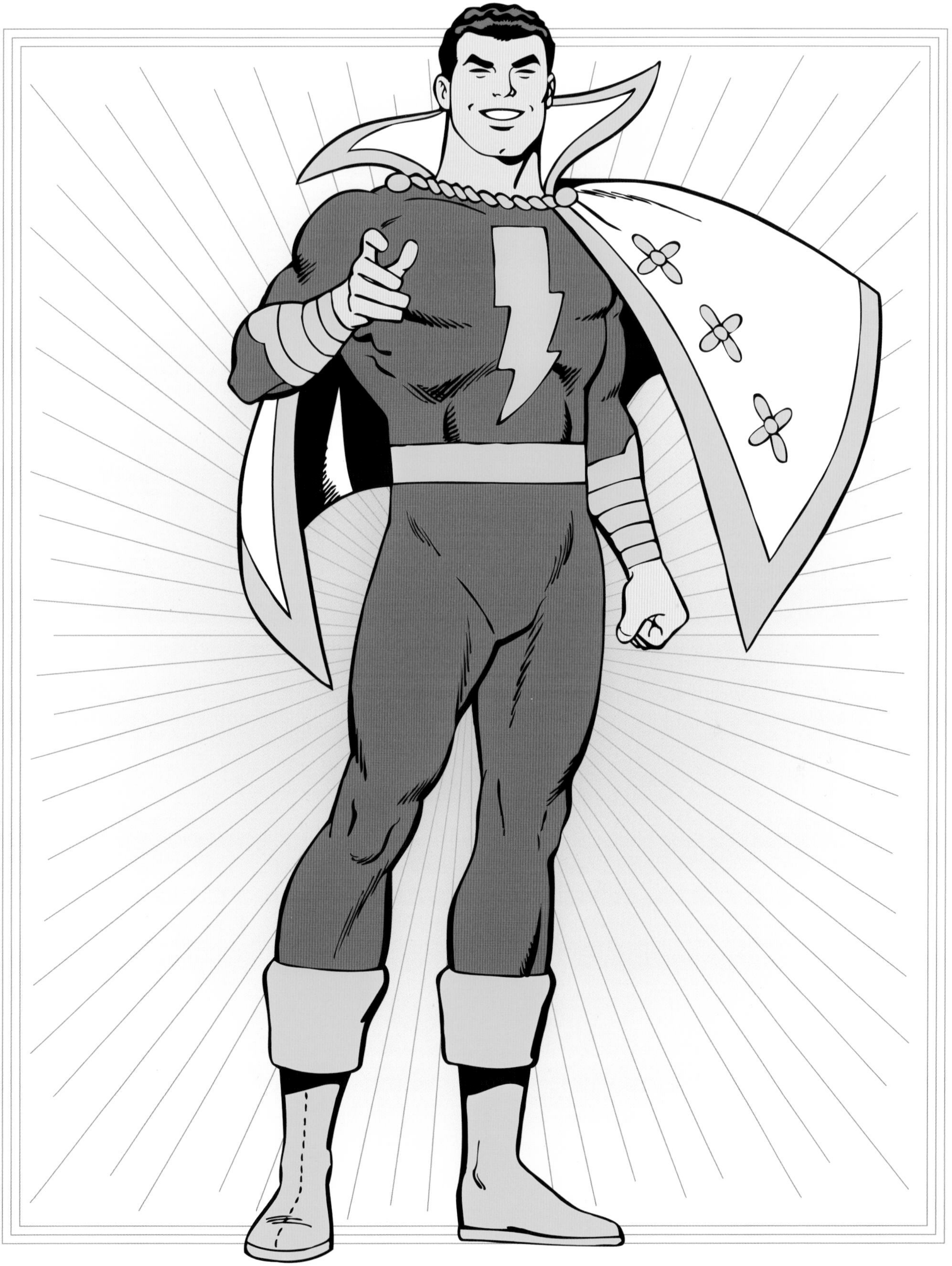

THE SHAZAM! FAMILY

Being a Super Hero is a lot of responsibility for a teenager. Billy quickly realized he could use some help protecting people. He also learned that he was able to share his powers. So in the same way that the old wizard shared his powers with Billy, Billy turned to the people he had grown to trust the most, his foster siblings.

Rosa and Victor Vasquez welcomed this group of teens into their home, and it was there that they all found family—with each other.

When the powers are shared, they're shared equally. So if only two siblings transform at once, they each have half the power that Billy would have if he was working solo. If all five siblings shout "Shazam!" at the same time, they each have one-fifth the strength of the full powers. Even then, they would be way stronger and faster than regular humans.

MARY

The oldest of the foster kids, Mary was really responsible and often took on the role of mothering the younger ones. Billy knew that Mary could be trusted to use her superpowers wisely.

EUGENE

Eugene was a tech and computer geek before he became a Super Hero. When he transforms, he has the additional power of technopathy. This means that he can communicate with and control machines and technology.

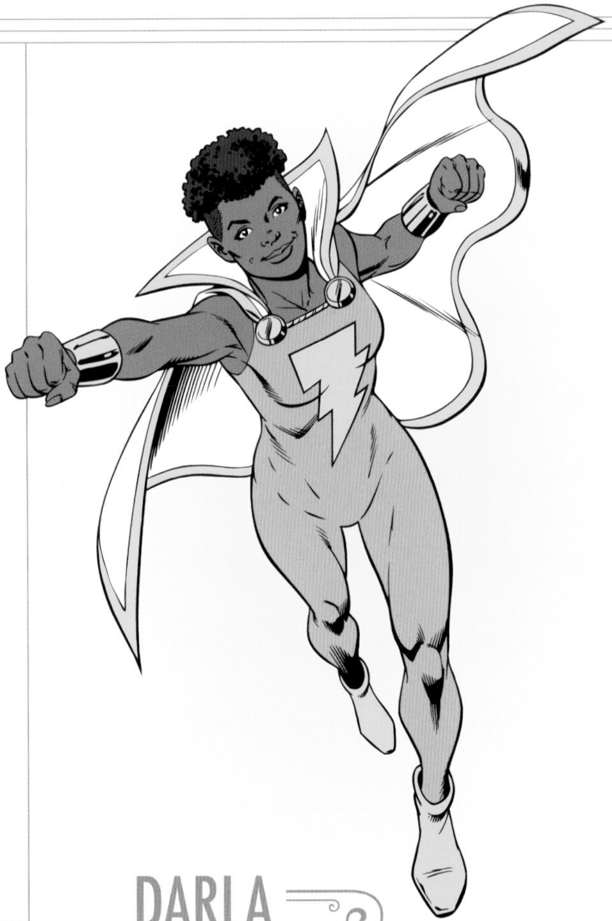

PEDRO

As a teenager, Pedro was self-conscious about his weight and size. As a Super Hero, Pedro has even greater super-strength than his siblings. When something needs that extra push, everyone turns to Pedro.

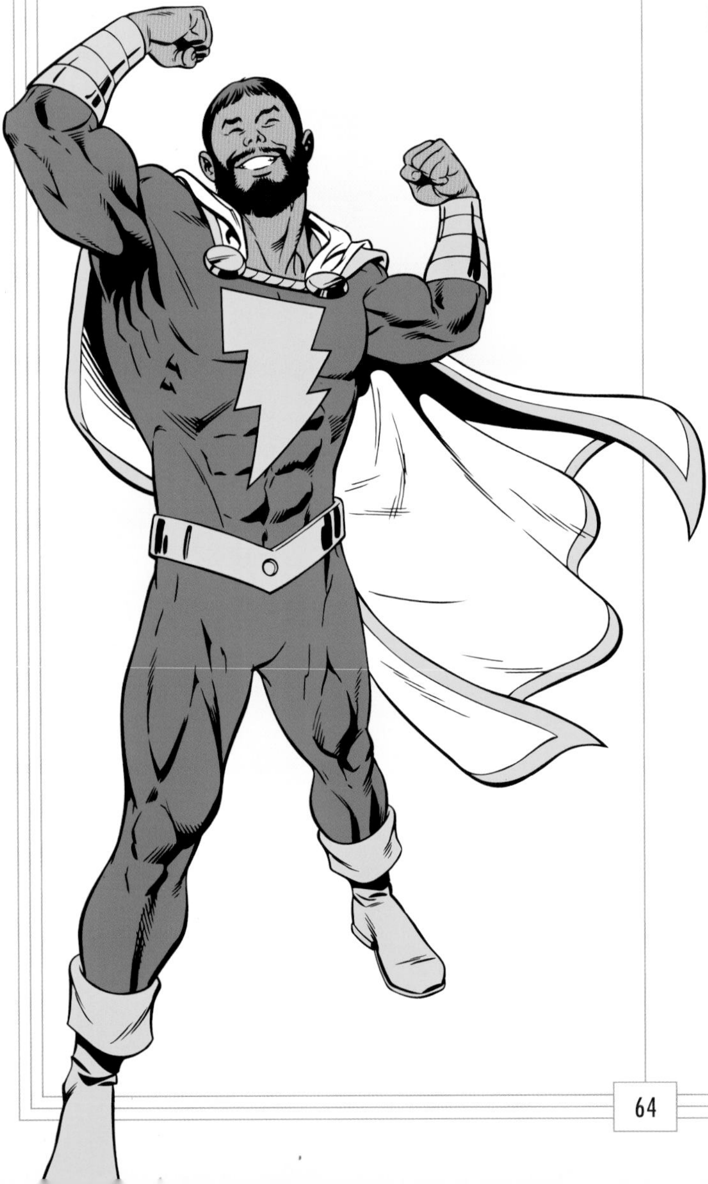

DARLA

Darla is the youngest and smallest of the group. In spite of a difficult childhood without her parents, she remained loving and friendly and kind to everyone she knew, especially her brothers and sister. When she slips into her purple costume and becomes a Super Hero, she is the fastest one of all. Darla has a hard time keeping secrets—she still has some maturing to do. It's not easy to be a Super Hero before you're even a teenager, and she does her best!